Mayhem in Monterey
The CIA, the Mafia, and the Yacht

Larry Andrews

ACKNOWLEDGMENTS

My wife Sue for always being there

Allen Lay for yacht racing advisement

Yohana Medina for plot development assistance

Millie Ames Writer's Workshop
for the critique during manuscript development

PROLOGUE

"Those CIA agents, they should die, both of them. They are responsible, I'm sure of it. I loved Franco. He was a good man. Angelina was a wonderful daughter and grew up to be a wonderful woman. You already know that. They must be avenged."

Adriana, recent widow of Franco Gambioni, Don of the largest of the five Mafia organized-crime families in New York, addressed the underboss, consigliere, and capos of the family. Her words were almost a command rather than a plea Her anger then turned to remorse, tears appearing as she began to sob. Nunzio, Franco's brother and a capo in the organization, consoled her and ushered her out of the room.

CHAPTER 1

MAY THEY REST IN PEACE

C IA Agents Marcus Peterson and Jenna Adams, though working in the same office in New York, literally met on their first assignment monitoring a Mafia crime boss on a Caribbean cruise. Teamed undercover as newlyweds, they developed a relationship. This subsequently matured during Marcus's second assignment in Tuscany, Italy. There, teamed with an MI6 agent, he was involved investigating a drug smuggling operation being carried out by Sicilian Mafiosi and a Colombian drug cartel.

Upon his return, he and Jenna felt it would be far more economical for both of them to move in together and share a residence. This turned out to be an apartment on the east side of Manhattan.

It was a Sunday morning. Marcus had just returned from a run through Central Park, picking up the New York Times on his way home. Jenna had prepared her first breakfast for the two of them. "Wow, I really never knew you could cook, Jenna, this looks really great," said Marcus as he settled down at the table.

"There are still probably many things you don't know about me, Marcus, but start eating; don't let the eggs get cold. I'll pour the coffee." Finishing the Western omelet and toast that Jenna had prepared, they both proceeded to drink their coffee and attack the *New York Times*. Marcus, deep into the sports page, was startled when Jenna called out, "Marcus, listen. There is a Gambioni obit in the paper for both Franco and daughter Angelina. 'Funeral to be held at St. Patrick's Cathedral, burial at St. John Cemetery in Queens.' Of course, there is no mention in the obit or the rest of the paper that Franco Gambioni hung himself in prison or that his daughter was shot when the FBI conducted a raid on the family's illegal cocaine smuggling operation. If you read the obit in its entirety, you would think it was just a normal Italian family that suffered a tragic loss." The Gambioni family had been the primary adversary in their past assignments.

"Do we dare go?" continued Jenna.

"Why should we?" replied Marcus.

"I guess I'm just a little curious."

"It could be a little dicey, but since it's being held at St. Patrick's, that implies a big crowd. We might be able to attend unobserved. St. John Cemetery is a bit of a tourist stop in New York as many past Mafia crime bosses are buried there. In fact, even tours are conducted. If it's crowded we might be able to go there undetected, but I don't think we would want the family to recognize us," responded Marcus.

Marcus and Jenna stood away from the crowd standing and seated at the burial site. They were close enough to hear, but not close enough to be considered part of the assembly. It was an unusual setting. Two coffins were to be lowered into the ground side by side. Seated at the gravesite was Adriana Gambioni, widow of the Mafia crime boss, Franco, and mother of their daughter, Angelina. On either side of her were Gambioni family members, none of whom Marcus and Jenna knew. They suspected that one was Franco's brother and the other his sister as listed in the obit as surviving members of the family.

"I couldn't believe the crowd at St. Patrick's," said Jenna. "I believe the majority of them were all members of the five Mafia families here in New York. It was interesting in that there was no receiving line after the service. The immediate family just exited forward. By the way, how does organized crime get away with using the Cathedral? Doesn't the Cardinal know they are all criminals?"

"Jenna, remember the Catholic Church teaches and believes all sins are forgiven by the Lord and any revenue, regardless of where it comes from, is graciously received," said Marcus softly with a slight smile on his face. "I am sure the Gambioni family made a major contribution for the service. Now as to a receiving line, there probably will be one at the reception being held at Trattoria l'Incontro, to which we are not going. I admit, I did have some feelings for Angelina on our first assignment on the Caribbean cruise, but that definitely vanished due to the many things that subsequently occurred. Like trying to kill us in the so-called accidental gas explosion and fire in the condo they wanted to loan us or the attempted assassination of me when on assignment in Tuscany." As Marcus continued talking, he gave Jenna's hand a little squeeze, reinforcing his total affection for her. "I often wonder whether Angelina and Adriana were aware of the price Franco put on my head with the local Mafia in San Gimignano."

Oh, it appears the services are about over. I suggest we quickly leave. I don't think Adriana spotted us either at the service or here, and it would be just as well if she didn't. I'm not sure who's going to run that family in the future but with Franco's death, we probably don't have to worry about his continued attempts to go after us for spying on them during the cruise. Come, Jenna, we have to pack. We have a plane to catch in the morning. It's off to California and the beginning of a new adventure." Marcus and Jenna had been teamed again together on a new operational assignment. Prior to embarking on that activity, they had been directed to report to the Defense Language Institute Foreign Language Center at the Presidio in Monterey, California.

As they turned to leave, they did not notice Adriana staring in their direction, then pointing at them and saying something to the brother-in-law sitting next to her. In her mind the sorrow she was suffering was all their fault and they should pay.

⟨ID⟩

At the reception Adriana cornered her brother-in-law Nunzio and in a very commanding voice said, "Remember that couple I pointed out to you at the gravesite? Well, they are the CIA Agents, Marcus Peterson and Jenna, that I spoke about at the family meeting. I don't know her last name. We spent 10 days on a cruise with them. They were posing as newlyweds and were literally spying on us. Well, as I said, I want them dead. I'm convinced in some way they are responsible for Franco and Angelina's demise. It should be some sort of a tragic accident. No way can we deal with a murder investigation. I'm sure they will be sent off on another mission together and as soon as they leave town, I want it to take place. Find out where they live and when they're sent off. Find out where they're going. I'm sure we have contacts."

In a somewhat pleading tone Nunzio responded, "Adriana, please. We are mourning and celebrating Franco and Angelina. Don't go there now."

You could see the rage in Adriana's face as she came back in a firm voice. "They should die, *capisce*?"

◐

Attending the Gambioni funeral provided somewhat a catharsis of their mindset concerning the interactions they had experienced with that organized crime family. All thoughts were now on their new assignment.

As they packed and prepared to go to the airport, Jenna and Marcus's conversation was all about the trip to California and the school that they were assigned to attend. "Jenna, have you ever been to California? I haven't been any further west than New Jersey. It's sort of weird; I have been as far east as Italy as have you but never west."

"Well, actually you have been further west than New Jersey. On the cruise we took we went to Cartagena, Colombia, and that is a bit further west than New Jersey. As for me, I have been to California. I applied to Berkeley and went there for a visit. When we found out the tuition and possible expenses, I settled for City College. By the way, while you were at admin picking up our orders, I went to travel and picked up our travel package. Very interesting. It's one way. They told me depending on issues that are currently being worked out, we may come back to New York after schooling or we may go directly to our next mission. They didn't say where our next mission was. Is there any indication on our orders?"

"No, they just say report to the Presidio and the language school. Nothing further. They wouldn't tell me anything either. So who knows where we go from there. I assume in good time we'll be told. Well, how are we going?"

"We fly nonstop to San Francisco on American on their 737 Max. That's their new center aisle plane. It could make the trip in less than 5 1/2 hours. At SFO we change to United Express into Monterey. It's only a little over 100 miles to Monterey, about an hour flight. We could've rented a car and driven. Not knowing the area, I thought it best to fly into Monterey and rent a car there. Travel didn't have a problem with that. By the way, we have about an hour and a half layover in SFO between flights. I have been in San Francisco airport and it is fairly new. It went through a major redo a few years back. We flew into there and drove over to Berkeley. There are plenty of places to eat there, and after a five-and-a-half hour flight, we'll probably be ready for lunch. I'm sure we only get a snack on the flight. I'm excited about Monterey. From the research I did on the net, there is a lot to do. There are a lot of vineyards and wineries in the area. You will think you are back in Italy."

Then seeing Marcus's face turn sad (he was obviously reflecting on the murder of two of their friends there) she tried to lighten the conversation. "Since we are just going to school, we should be able to do a little exploring. It's going to be great, Marcus. Try and forget our past assignments and look at this as a sort of vacation. I had the option to book us in one of the hotels that exist behind the gates on the Presidio or in town. I elected in town. I thought we could play tourist when not going to school."

"It's interesting, Jenna, our orders only say report to the language school in Monterey. No mention of what we're going to do there or where we're going to go afterwards," said Marcus.

"Well, let me fill you in," said Jenna. "The gal at the travel office was very informative. She had not been there, but she has prepared several travel packages to go there and gotten feedback from many who have been there. According to her we will not be briefed on what our follow-on mission will be until we report. For security reasons this is never put on paper. Based on our follow-on mission, our program will be set up.

The program can be quite involved. In learning the language of wherever we're going, we have to learn to speak it with proper inflections, write and read it, and understand it when it's spoken to us. Further, we will be taught all about the culture. That would include gestures that you would normally use in conversation. The school's goal is to transform us into appearing as a local of the country we are going to."

"Oh boy, this could be rough," responded Marcus. "Language wasn't my best effort in either high school or college."

"Well, that's the other fascinating issue. By the way, I wasn't that great on language either. The time we spend there is a function of how we progress. Evidently we're graded periodically on everything that we're learning and until we achieve a proper score we are not deployed. So basically, how long we're in Monterey is a function of how fast we learn."

"This doesn't sound like much of a vacation. By the way, where are we staying?"

"That's also intriguing. Currently we have reservations in the Monterey hotel in old town. It's close to Fisherman's Wharf and several of the hotels in the area. But that will only be temporary. Again, based on our assigned program and the current population of the school, we could be assigned housing on base. That comes in different varieties. There is basic military housing and there are some 37 historical houses that have been upgraded and are available. They supposedly are in walking distance to the classes. I expect that's the luck of the draw, if we get assigned there.

As far as the vacation, yes, based on what she told me, the whole program sounds pretty intense but I'm sure we'll have some free time to be able to do a little exploring in the area."

CHAPTER 2

THE WELCOMING

C oncerned about the possible delay in security, Marcus and Jenna arrived at the airport about an hour before flight time. Jenna had not shown Marcus their tickets until they got to the American counter. Marcus was pleasantly surprised. "Business class, we are certainly on up-scale travel," said Marcus.

"Yes, and I have another surprise for you," said Jenna. "Travel gave us a guest card to the Admirals Club so we will not be waiting with the masses for our plane."

After checking in, they proceeded directly to the Admirals Club. Jenna passed the guest card along with their tickets to the receptionist and they both were surprised when she said, "Welcome, Mr. & Mrs. Peterson. I have a package for you. It was delivered earlier this morning."

Recognizing the envelope, Jenna said, "It's from the office. I bet it's our follow-on orders."

Settling down at adjacent chairs in the club, Jenna opened the envelope and was surprised to see a single sheet of paper with bullet instructions and a paragraph at the top in red, stating, "This document should be destroyed upon reading." They both stared at the document and then slowly read it out loud in a quiet whisper.

- **Your cover off base:**
  - **You are a married couple.**
  - **You work at the UN.**
  - **You have been sent to Monterey to learn some additional languages, a normal requirement of your job.**
- **You will remain at the Monterey hotel until instructed differently by the school.**
- **On Wednesday morning you will proceed to the Transit Plaza in old Monterey and board the Military bus that you will see there at 8 AM sharp. This will transport you to the Presidio and check-in.**

Enjoy your trip.

"Marcus, there's a shredder in the business room with the computers. I suggest we put this in there now. It's pretty straightforward and I think we can remember our marching orders."

⟪Φ⟫

As they settled in their seats on the plane Jenna said, "I don't know if you noticed I was staring at the crowd while we were boarding and I could swear I saw a double for that man we saw sitting next to Adriana at the burial. The one we thought was Franco's brother. He was clean-shaven, as opposed to the one we saw who had a slight beard, but he sure looked like a twin. Obviously, as business class, we boarded early and I couldn't see whether he was boarding our plane or was just in the general area."

"They say everybody has a look-alike. I wouldn't worry about it. Put it out of your mind. Let's enjoy the flight," responded Marcus. The 5 1/2 hour flight went fast; actually, it was six hours due to headwinds. Between lunch being served and watching a movie, they both were surprised when the announcement came over the intercom to fasten seatbelts in preparation for landing at SFO. *P.A.*

Quick directions at the gate sent them off to the Admirals Club. "Jenna, this is fabulous. It's another enjoyable lounge to kick back in while we wait for our next flight. Things just couldn't be better," said Marcus as they settled into adjoining chairs in the lounge.

⨁

LiJing Chen had been recruited in Hong Kong to teach at the Defense Language Institute Foreign Language Center at the Presidio. Her father worked at the US Consulate in Hong Kong and during her schooling at the University she worked part-time as an intern there. Being fluent in Cantonese and Mandarin, as well as English, it was felt that she would be an asset to the language school.

The recruitment had taken place when the British turned over Hong Kong to mainland China. Her father encouraged her to take the offered position as he was not too sure what the future held in Hong Kong under Chinese rule. As issues began to develop between the US and China, more members of the military and government agencies were being sent to the language school at the Presidio to learn Mandarin. After a 20-year tenure at the school she was beginning to plan retirement. Due to her unique capabilities and their needs, retirement was being discouraged by the school's management.

Shortly after she had been recruited and moved to California, her father had been transferred to the US Consulate in Singapore. Thus, through the years she had spent considerable time in Singapore on family visits. Putting a program together to school candidates in life in Southeast Asia, primarily Hong Kong and Singapore, was easy and most enjoyable for her. This was evident by student feedback. All claimed she made a very difficult program not only a challenge but enjoyable.

⨁

The flight into Monterey from San Francisco was short and on approach Marcus, looking out the plane window, commented, "Jenna, this is smaller than Teterboro airport in New Jersey and I thought that was a small airport. I flew into there once. This is really small. When they hold the golf tournament at Pebble Beach, I wonder how many fly into Monterey."

"Oh, I'm sure most people just fly into San Francisco and drive down, but we're here and it should be fun. I could see the budget car rental sign on approach. It's right next to the terminal. We should be in old town Monterey in no time."

⦿

Monterey hotel had an old section that had been there for years and a brand-new connecting section recently built. The entire hotel consisted primarily of suites, some larger, some smaller. Check-in was at a small counter in the old hotel lobby. It had a feeling that you were dropping back in time. There was a small seating area with a fireplace that gave you quite a cozy feeling. As they walked into the area, they were both totally surprised as a middle-aged man got up from a chair, walked over and put his arms around Jenna saying, "Welcome to Monterey."

"Uncle Mark, what are you doing here? How did you know we were coming? And driving over to welcome us! What a pleasant surprise. It's been a long time."

"Your parents called me and gave me your itinerary. I thought it only fitting I should come greet you."

Jenna, then turning to Marcus, said, "This is my Uncle Mark Jones. He lives in Salinas and I was going to look him up. I haven't really seen him since I was a kid."

Looking at Marcus, Mark Jones said, "I work at the aquarium and stopping here to greet you was easy due to it being on my way home. I wanted to welcome you and give you directions to my house and our phone number. Hopefully we can get together. I understand you're attending the language school here and from what I hear, it's pretty demanding. But please, if you have any free time, give us a call and we can get together. I know your Aunt Susan would love to see you. And also, if you need any help or any assistance or anything like that, don't hesitate to call. I have to run along now, as traffic really gets rough on that single-lane road east to Salinas at this time of night. Please give us a call when you get a chance. Oh, and you've got to come to the aquarium. It's the best in the country. I'd love to show you around." With that last comment and another hug with Jenna, Mark was gone.

Marcus, turning to Jenna, said, "That's pretty exciting, having a relative close by. Not too bad and I'd love to see that aquarium. I heard a lot about it from some of the others at the office who have been out here."

"I hope this doesn't get us in trouble," said Jenna. "I guess I shouldn't have told my parents where we were going and what we were going to do. I had to tell them something as we were leaving town."

"Not to worry, Jenna, we just use our basic cover that we were told in the assignment orders that we destroyed. Let's get checked in. We can deal with this later."

⊕

After settling in, and on advice from the hotel, they proceeded to walk towards Fisherman's Wharf for a seafood dinner. It seemed like the proper way to celebrate their arrival in Monterey. They had completed the two-block walk toward the entrance to Fisherman's Wharf and were crossing Main Street when someone yelled, "Look out!" They jumped to the curb seconds before a red Tesla zoomed past them.

"Holy shit, that could've killed us," said Jenna. "Whoever it was, he or she driving was speeding, and I didn't hear a thing."

"You wouldn't. It was a Tesla electric car. Powered by electric motors, they are very quiet," said Marcus.

"And they have self-driving capability," said the gentleman walking up to them who had warned them to jump out of the way. "The rental car company here is trying out these self-driving cars and it's causing chaos. Damn lucky you didn't get hit. I would file a complaint with the car agency," he said, continuing with, "You didn't see it, but there was no one in the car. Somehow it was programmed to go somewhere with no one in it, and obviously at a rapid speed It could've killed you both."

"Thanks for saving our lives," said Marcus.

"Be careful walking around the streets in old town. This is not the first time one of those cars has gone awry."

"Thanks again," said Marcus, and they continued on their way to Fisherman's Wharf.

As they entered the area, Marcus was amazed. "Look at all the shops and restaurants crammed into this really small wharf. It will be hard to determine where to eat," he said.

"Not to worry, Marcus. Fred, my friend over at the FBI, has been out here several times and his main comment to me was that you've got to go to Abalonetti's Bar and Grill. It's really great and known for its calamari, but it also serves other seafood. It's out near the end of the wharf."

"What's calamari and when did you tell Fred we were coming out here?"

"Calamari is another name for squid and don't make a face, you're going to love it, I guarantee. Now about Fred. When we saw the obit in the paper about the Gambioni funeral, I called to ask if he was going. I forgot to mention it. I think you were in the shower at the time. That's when I told him we would be going to Monterey language school and he came back with all sorts of comments about Monterey, where we should go, and what we should see. He rambled on so fast that I couldn't get half of it. But I do remember him saying that Abalonetti's on Fisherman's Wharf would be the best seafood place to go to. I'm sure we'll see it to try it out, but we can certainly try many more. Look, every one of the restaurants here has a little stand out front offering you a free sample of their clam chowder. I guess it's a good way to taste each one's version. This first place, the Crab House, let's start."

Marcus and Jenna worked their way down the wharf and eventually got to Abalonetti's, where they got seated at a nice table next to the windows looking out at the bay. They had just had their wine served when Jenna's cell phone rang. "Who could be calling me?" she said out loud, and then looking at her phone said, "It's my friend, Fred."

"Take the call," said Marcus.

"Hi Fred, what's up? You're kidding. Thanks for the warning. We might've experienced their first attempt, and we will keep in touch. I assume you have a local operation out here. Good. Text me and Marcus a contact name and number. That way we'll both have it on our phones. Thanks much."

Clicking off the phone and looking at Marcus's anticipating face, Jenna said, "You wouldn't believe. I thought we were going to enjoy our so-called vacation and our past would be behind us. Well, unfortunately it's not going to be true. The word on the street, and you know Fred has contacts with all the local Mafia organized-crime families, is that Adriana has ordered us to be accidentally taken out. Based on what we just experienced, I think the first attempt was made."

"Well, if this is true, I would guess it's to be accomplished by someone sent from New York. I don't believe there's any love or relationship between New York Mafia and the West Coast organized crime. Italian organized crime primarily existed in Los Angeles area and San Francisco. The predominant organized crime families are either Mexican or Eurasian with Mexican families dealing primarily in drugs and the Eurasian families concentrating more on fraud. Right now, I don't think there's much we can do except to be aware.

"Now let's get back to enjoying our first meal in Monterey. Should I order the 'Fried Monterey Calamari'? The menu says it has been voted as the best in Monterey." asked Marcus.

"But of course," replied Jenna.

⟨I⟩

After a brief breakfast provided by the hotel, Jenna and Marcus were off to the local Transit Plaza. This was really just a parking area where several local buses parked and left from, and was only three blocks away from the hotel. Arrival presented them with several buses but one conspicuous by its military colors and markings.

"There is our bus as forecasted," said Marcus. The staff sergeant standing by the bus inspected their travel orders before allowing them onboard.

"Well, our adventure is about to begin," said Jenna, as they settled themselves in the only two seats together available on the bus.

It was a short drive to the Presidio gate and before they knew it, they were disembarking the bus and entering an administrative building. There they were processed, which included giving them badges depicting their name and picture. After processing, they were directed to one of five conference rooms where they were greeted by LiJing Chen. They were the last of the 10 assigned that room and as soon as they were seated, LiJing began her introductory speech.

"Ladies and gentlemen, welcome to the Presidio. I am LiJing Chen and will be your instructor, guardian, and commanding officer during your entire stay. According to your orders, you have been assigned to group SH10 or SH11. If you look at the badges that were issued you, you will see that number directly below your name. Hopefully, when we are done with you, you will be fluent in Mandarin Chinese and Malay languages. Further, you will be comfortable displaying physical and emotional attributes of someone who has spent their entire life living in Southeast Asia. There will be classroom training, and there will be projects involving competition between teams 10 and 11. Most all activities will take place in the confines of the Presidio. The team activities will involve escape rooms that will become configured considerably different than you probably have ever been exposed to before. There will be three of these projects during the program. The first will be about 1/3 into the program and all written clues in the escape room will be in *kanji* and you will be required to only communicate in Mandarin. The competition will be which team can escape first. The second project will occur about two-thirds into the program and it will be similar to the first, but everything will be in Malay language. The last project will be somewhat complicated. The clues in the escape room will be in English, Malay and Mandarin. Further, members of the team will only be allowed to communicate in a specific language. At that point in time, each member of the team will be assigned a specific language to communicate in. Obviously, this will create an environment to simulate your future assignment.

"As I mentioned before, you are part of a unique class and we will be utilizing a different approach to your learning. Normally participants are involved in total immersion, exposing them to an environment where all communication is in the language they are learning to speak. Because your future assignment involves locations where English is the predominant language but is the second language of most locals, your training will be different. We have been directed to prepare you to become as close as possible to a southeast Asian that has a native language of Mandarin Chinese or Malay. As such, starting in one month's time, all activity on the Presidio will be total immersion. First will be in Mandarin Chinese. Then Malay. We will not move to Malay until we are totally pleased with your progress in Chinese. Residing off base, you will be in a normal English environment. Ultimately you should be able to mix languages in conversation as most locals do depending on whom they are conversing with. The overall program usually involves 18 months to two years. However, in your case, we will endeavor to shorten it, possibly to six to eight months. It will be a function of how you progress. The expanded section of the Monterey hotel has condominiums and the married couples among you will be moved there as soon as vacancies are available. The rest of you single students will be moved to barracks at Fort Ord."

As LiJing continued to describe the program that was about to occur, Jenna, looking down at both their badges whispered to Marcus, "We are on separate teams. Competition could be fun." The rest of the day went pretty smoothly. Jenna and Marcus mingled with the other members of their class getting to know them. They were issued several books and given reading assignments to be accomplished over the weekend. They were told that if they were living off base, they could continue to do that until instructed otherwise.

When five o'clock rolled around, they all couldn't exit fast enough, rushing to the waiting bus. On the drive back into town Jenna commented, "I really felt I was back in college. I think this is going to be pretty demanding."

"I agree," said Marcus. "I don't know about you, but I can't wait for a libation to relax with. Let's stop in at the Alvarado Street Brewery & Grill. It's close to our hotel and everybody says it's the place to go."

⟐

In a federal prison southeast of Monterey, a high-ranking member of La eMe (the local Mexican Mafia) spoke to his daughter on his illegal cell phone. "Yohana, it's time for you to go sailing again. I will text you the coordinates and expected time where you will meet the cartel shipment. After the cargo transfer, return to your mooring in Monterey Bay Marina. Secure the boat, stowing the sails and installing the deck covers. Leave the hatch doors and the main cabin unlocked."

Before Yohana could respond, the phone went dead. This was not unusual as cell phones were not allowed in prisons. The illegal ones that existed were passed around surreptitiously and hid whenever guards were present.

Yohana's sailboat was a 40' ketch-rigged Newporter, with a 13' beam. It had an auxiliary diesel which provided for a 900-mile cruising range if wind was light and fluky. It was called *Spirit*, a beautiful cruising craft that had been completely restored with new equipment in the past five years. Yohana was known locally as a proficient sailor. A member of the Monterey Peninsula Yacht Club, she participated in many of the local regattas, often recruiting her crew from local college girls. She lived with her mother and older brother in a small house on the Latinx side of Monterey. She worked as a hostess at the Sardine Factory restaurant while her brother was a caddie at Pebble Beach. They both never appeared to lack resources to participate in the many activities in Monterey. This caused many to be curious as to where the money came from as both jobs certainly didn't pay that well.

⊕

Marcus completed his run, round trip from Fisherman's Wharf to the aquarium, on the Monterey Bay Coastal trail. Walking up to Crab Louie's Bistro on the wharf, where he expected to meet Jenna for breakfast, he was surprised to see most all other restaurants were closed but just beginning to open and prepare for the daily operation. Looking across at the yacht harbor, he saw many people on their boats, raising sails, and preparing to take them out. One rather large sailboat, a Newporter ketch, caught his eye. It was too large for the normal slips and was moored at the end of the harbor strip that accommodated multiple facing slips for smaller craft. Whether it was the size of the boat or the attractive female in a bikini who was setting sails that caught his eye, he really homed in on the boat. It was close enough that he could read its name on the stern, *Spirit*. *I'll have to ask about this. Maybe somebody in the restaurant knows more,* he said to himself.

As he entered the restaurant, he spotted Jenna sitting at a window table wolfing down a crab benedict. "I'm sorry, Marcus. I was so hungry I just couldn't wait," she said as Marcus sat down.

He commented, "Who are your friends," pointing to the two pelicans sitting on the wharf just outside the window preening their feathers.

"I was so hungry I read the menu, ordered and got right into my meal. I can't believe I missed them. They're right outside and seem to be oblivious of us being so close. I guess they can't see in the window. Goodness, look at all the activity on the boats. It looks like today is boat day."

"Yes, it looks like they're having some sort of a yacht race today," he said. "We'll have to ask the waitress about it. It could be fun to watch. By the way, my run was great. That coastal trail is almost completely level, with historical markers along the way, one of which explained why it was so level. It used to be the tracks for the railroad that existed to transport the sardine shipments from the processing plants on Cannery Row. There is so much to see here, I just hope we get enough free time to explore. Before I forget, there are lots more places to eat on Cannery

Row before you get to the Aquarium. It's not that bad a walk so we can certainly consider going there to eat in addition to Fisherman's Wharf and Alvarado Street."

As the waitress took Marcus's order, she answered his questions, saying, "This is just one of the many summer and fall yacht regattas that are held every year. Some involve the yacht club up in Santa Cruz. They will be sailing out in the bay. You really have to be up on high to see what's going on once they get out there. I would suggest you go up by the Presidio Museum, as the bluff is high enough there and it looks out over the bay. It would be ideal for watching the regatta. As to the large ketch, it's owned by the Mendez family. Their daughter Yohana and her brother Juan usually do the sailing. After the race most all congregate over at the Monterey Peninsula Yacht Club on the other wharf. They will present the awards and have a big party. I dated Yohana's brother, Juan, for a while and got to go to the party one year. Lots of fun."

⊕

That afternoon they toured the Monterey Peninsula, driving the 17-mile drive that goes through Pacific Grove, Pebble Beach and ends at Carmel. It was late afternoon when they got back to Fisherman's Wharf and thought a cup of chowder at Abalonetti's would be in order. Parking and walking out on the pier they saw all the sailboats coming back in.

"The race must be over," said Marcus. "They all seem to be coming back in."

"Yes, but I don't see any sign of that large sailboat you like so much."

"No, neither do I. I wonder where it went. Maybe after the race it went up to Santa Cruz or out in the ocean. It's certainly large enough; it could go just about anywhere it wants. I guess we have to assume it was not in the competition. Otherwise, they definitely would've returned to see if they won."

⊕

The sea was calm as the ketch *Spirit* dropped all sails and started its diesel engine. "I see her," said Yohana as she peered through her binoculars looking south. "She's slowing down and should be here momentarily. Juan, prepare to throw them a line. We must lash together and transfer the cargo as quickly as possible. This calm sea may not last."

19

The sleek *Picuda* smuggling vehicle slowed to a drift as it approached *Spirit*. Lashed together, the ton of cocaine was transferred quickly. *Picuda* was released and headed south at great speed. Yohana and Juan set sail on *Spirit* heading back to Monterey Bay.

CHAPTER 3

STRANGE PARTNERS

B y the following week of classes, Marcus and Jenna became considerably attached to the Wong family. They were the only other students in the group of ten that appeared to be a couple and they also were residing at the Monterey Hotel. Jack Wong's parents were from Taiwan and he was fluent in Cantonese, while his wife Sofia was of Brazilian background so had a second language of Portuguese. An interesting couple who worked for the State Department, they currently called Chicago their home. Sunday, they had gone out to dinner together on Cannery Row at the Fish Hopper Restaurant.

They also were on separate teams. Jack was on Jenna's team and Sophia on Marcus's team and they joked about the upcoming competition, not having any idea of what would be involved. Walking back to the hotel from the bus stop, they were surprised to find Alvarado Street, where the hotel was, completely blocked off and filled with all sorts of booths.

"Oh yea," said Sophia. "It's a farmers market. They told me about this at the front desk. It happens every Tuesday evening with all sorts of fresh farm vegetables as well as booths selling flowers, food, trinkets, you name it. This should be fun. We get to tour it on the way home."

Blocked off streets were filled with people shopping as well as just browsing. It appeared to be locals as well as tourists and students. There were street entertainers also along the three-block run, so overall the noise level was quite high.

Marcus stopped at a booth selling English toffee and was busily tasting the product when Jenna came up, pulled on his sleeve, and whispered in his ear. "Marcus, I know you're not going to believe this, but in the crowd just a few minutes ago, I spotted that same guy that I saw back in the terminal in New York, the one I thought looked like Franco's brother. I wonder if he could be the nemesis that Fred was warning us about. Maybe we should tell the Wongs about our predicament. They know we're CIA, but they certainly don't know that somebody's trying to kill us. I don't want to endanger them."

"Oh, come on Jenna, how can that be true. That was back in New York. We are in Monterey, California, and have traveled across county on two different airlines. It's dark and lighting is poor. Recognizing somebody in this environment has really got to be questionable. I think you're just a little hyper based on the phone call we got from Fred. If it'll make you feel better, we can certainly tell the Wongs. For now, just enjoy the street fair."

⊕

Nunzio Gambioni sat outside Starbucks on Alvarado Street in Monterey, speaking on a cell phone to Adriana. "Adriana, I think we should drop this whole matter. This is not the place or the time to accomplish what you desire. Let's just drop it. I want to come back home to New York."

"What do you mean, it's not the place? I told you I want them dead. Now," screamed Adriana over the phone.

"Adriana, you don't understand. This is a small town. It's not like New York City and we have no family here. The community is filled with military and all sorts of government personnel, attending schools, etc. Out here, I just don't feel comfortable in this environment and I certainly don't want to try orchestrating a murder that appears to be an accidental death."

"Nunzio, this is a family vendetta. Do what is required. *Capisce?*" And the phone went dead.

Damn that woman! Accomplishing what she wants could cost me my life. She's got to be out of her mind, thought Nunzio as he put his phone away.

⊕

The Petersons and the Wongs shared a table in the breakfast room which normally didn't open until seven. They had made arrangements with the hotel to be down there at 6:30 every morning to allow them to have a breakfast before they had to be on the bus to the Presidio, which left at 7:15 sharp.

All four had developed a little bit of routine. Jenna and Sophia made themselves waffles while Jack and Marcus toasted bagels. All conversation was about the anticipated change in activities in the future. "I'm not sure what to anticipate," said Jenna. "What is total immersion?"

"It means all conversation on base will be in Mandarin but that won't occur for at least two or three months. Our instructor and any base personnel that we associate with will only speak Mandarin. They in turn will not respond to our English. We must try to communicate as best we can in Mandarin," answered Marcus. "It will be difficult at first, but theoretically it will get easier each day."

"I find that hard to believe," said Sophia. "We have been married five years and I've been exposed to Cantonese every time I visit Jack's folks and I still can't understand what they're saying to me."

"It's probably just as well," said Jack with a smile on his face.

"Let's just say we're in for an interesting future," said Marcus, and then looking directly at Jack and Sophia, he continued, "Seriously, we want to caution you both. We have been alerted by the FBI in New York of a possible danger." He then related to them briefly the details of the Gambioni crime family and the vendetta they supposedly had laid on them.

⊕

During the next three months their activities were somewhat routine but heavily concentrated on learning Mandarin. It was school all day long, studying at night and on the weekends. Very little time was available for pleasure. What little pleasure they had was the occasional outing for dinner at one of the many restaurants.

They were well into the third month when on the weekend they decided to really splurge. Marcus had made reservations at the Sardine Factory, one of the most famous and expensive restaurants on Cannery Row. Not mentioning it to the others, Marcus was extremely excited. He had not forgotten what he was told about the attractive young sailor he had spotted in the marina on their early days in Monterey. *At last,* he thought, *I will finally get to meet the young sailor on the large sailboat we saw when we first arrived. She was extremely attractive and obviously very proficient sailing in those regattas, and there have been three since we have been here. She never returns with the other yachts, yet somehow she must return at night because we don't see the boat until next morning. There's got to be a story here.*

When they arrived and were being seated by Yohana, Marcus casually mentioned to her that he had seen her on the 40-foot ketch that he spotted in the marina. She thanked him for observing but immediately turned to the rest of the party, telling them to follow her as she led them through the crowded restaurant to their assigned table. Before they arrived at the table, Marcus tried once more to engage in conversation, saying, "What little we watched of the regattas you appear to handle her quite well. I'm also a sailor and I've raced in Long Island Sound on the East Coast with my father's 35-foot sloop."

"Thank you, again," she replied, "but I'm much too busy for conversation. Please be seated." And with that she left them at their table. They were well into their meal when Marcus spotted Yohana not busy as traffic in and out of the restaurant had appeared to slow. Addressing the table, he said, "I will give it another shot. I'd sure like to know something more about her and her sailboat."

"Oh Marcus, please!" said Jenna with a stern expression on her face. Before she could say anything more, Marcus was up and walking over to Yohana. As he approached, she asked, "Is there something wrong?"

"No, not at all. I just wanted to ask you a few more questions about sailing," responded Marcus.

"I'm sorry, Sir," she said, "Please return to your table. Management does not like me conversing with the patrons," and with that, she turned around and walked away.

Marcus, a little frustrated, returned to the table saying, "Well, so much for that. She obviously doesn't want to discuss sailing or anything else with patrons and that convinces me that there's some sort of a story here."

"What do you mean?" asked Jack. "Why are you so interested?"

"I guess it's just my CIA training," responded Marcus. "I have participated in many sailing races back on the East Coast and at the completion of the race all boats return to the beginning. It's not only the camaraderie, it's the judging, you want to know who won, who was disqualified, etc. The fact that they don't and the fact that we don't see that boat until the next morning tells me there's something unusual about what's happening, that's all."

"Marcus, we're not on duty here," said Jenna. "Enjoy your meal." There was annoyance displayed on her face and her thoughts were, *Is he getting bored with married life and looking for another playmate or is this really about what the sailboat is really doing? Is he thinking that the marriage we did in Gretna Green was not for real? This is upsetting.*

CHAPTER 4

STRANGE CARGO

J enna and Marcus finally broke free of their routine and spent the afternoon with Jenna's uncle Mark and wife Susan in Salinas. Marcus consumed considerable wine at dinner that evening and when the time to return to Monterey arrived, he looked at Jenna saying, "Maybe you better drive, Jenna. That two-lane road back to Monterey is bad enough in daylight, but in the dark I don't think I'm quite up to it."

After thank yous and goodbyes, Jenna and Marcus hopped in the car and started back home "I don't think we need the GPS," said Jenna. "It's a straight shot back." By the time she had driven out of Salinas and was on the main road back to Monterey, Marcus was sound asleep. *Well, so much for conversation to keep me awake,* she thought.

The drive was uneventful. Jenna had the radio on a music station and Marcus remained fast asleep. They had just pulled off Highway 1, proceeding into Monterey when Jenna yelled out, "Oh shit, I forgot to stay in the left lane. Damn it, we're going to be going to the marina instead of town."

"What's going on?" asked Marcus as he woke up.

"I was in the wrong lane and we are headed to the marina instead of downtown," replied Jenna.

"Not a problem," said Marcus. "Just drive into the marina parking lot and at the other end it will put you out within a block of Alvarado and we will be back to our hotel."

As they pulled into the marina parking lot, Marcus said, "Slow down. Look over by the boats. It's all dark except by the big ketch. There are lights on it and it looks like some people are on deck. Quick, stop the car, turn out the lights. Look, it appears they are offloading something and those doing it don't appear to be Yohana or her brother."

"Marcus, we have no business here. Let's go on."

"Jenna, isn't it a little strange for people to be working on a yacht and unloading stuff at 11 o'clock at night? I'll tell you my CIA training says we should take a look at what's going on. And if it looks suspicious, we can at least report it to local authorities. Come on. Let's see if we can get closer," said Marcus as he got out of their car.

They had just started walking to the docks in the parking lot when a stranger stepped out from behind a car holding a gun and said, "Where do you think you're going?" Marcus started to respond.

Jenna, noticing their adversary was not looking at her but looking at Marcus and also seeing that the gun he held had no silencer with one swift stroke of her right fist went directly at the throat of their adversary. He dropped his gun, grabbed for his neck and fell to the ground, choking. Jenna quickly picked up the gun, grabbed Marcus's arm, saying "Back to the car, we're out of here."

⌖

Safely back at the Monterey hotel, Marcus said, "Jenny, you were outstanding in the parking lot. Where did you learn that maneuver?"

"Angelina taught it to me on our Caribbean trip. It's a maneuver she learned in her karate class in college. Remember, that's how she got away from her kidnappers in San Juan. This was the first I tried it. I knew he wasn't going to shoot us, as there was no silencer on the gun he held and I didn't think they would like the noise of the shot going off. I thought we should get out of there right away as it's a tricky move. If you hit the throat too fast you could crush the larynx and the adversary dies.

I don't know whether I killed him or momentarily choked him. Have you any idea what they were loading or unloading from the boat?"

"We were pretty far away, but it sure looked like cocaine bricks. Maybe it's just my suspicious nature and I saw what I wanted to see. We obviously won't find out but we should definitely report to somebody."

"I can either call my Uncle Mark or maybe Fred back in New York."

"Let's go with Fred. He did say he had some contacts out here."

"Good point. It's 3 o'clock in the morning his time. We can wait till morning."

"By the way, what made you pick up our adversary's gun and where is it?"

"Oh, I'm sorry, it's in my purse. Let me get it for you. It's a Beretta handgun. Just like the one that Martina gave you in Italy. With a Mafia price on our heads, I thought you would feel better armed." As Jenna went for her purse, Marcus's brain went into overdrive with flashbacks: first, his shooting of the adversary that tried to kill him in his London apartment and second, the killing by a sniper, of Interpol Agent Martina Bufalino, who he befriended in Italy. Both actions occurred on his last mission.

⟨D⟩

As they settled into bed, what had just occurred began to have its effect on Jenna. Her brave, calm and serious way dissolved. Curling up in a fetal position she began to shake and whimper. Marcus immediately jumped in bed and cradled her. He could feel the tenseness in her body. Gently stroking her and speaking softly to calm her, he said, "Easy, my love. You will be fine. You did well, we are not hurt. All will be good."

She slowly began to relax and Marcus switched from holding her tight to gently caressing her body. Brushing his fingers along her arm, her cheek, her neck, and running downward along the curve of her waist and hips, then slipping his hand under her nightgown. She turned toward him and he continued to gently caress her, brushing his hand along the skin below her navel and then stroking back up around the curves of her breasts and along her ribs. She pulled his head towards her breasts and they ultimately made passionate love before falling sound asleep.

⟨D⟩

Waking early the next morning, Marcus rolled over, kissing Jenna lightly on the nose to wake her and said, "Jenna, last night was wonderful. Crime, then passion. That could be an exciting lifestyle."

Jenna smiled, throwing her arms around Marcus saying, "Let's just go for the latter, and you get the shower first." As soon as Marcus was out of bed, Jenna was on the phone. "Hi, Fred, I'm glad I caught you. 6:30 here; it must be 9:30 in New York. Look, we experienced an issue last night that I thought I better check with you before I contact anyone out here about it. I was going to call one of the numbers you texted us, but Marcus thought I better talk to you first. Oh, also, I might have killed someone"

"Well, that got my attention. What's the story?" Jenna described in detail what they experienced the previous night. By this time Marcus was out of the shower and on the other extension in their suite.

"Hi, Fred. Marcus here. I'm on the extension. I guess if Jenna's fist to the guy caused him to choke to death, we're home free. I don't believe anyone else saw us. If he didn't die, it was dark enough. I don't believe he could recognize us. I'm saying this because even though he was in front of us and holding a gun, I could barely see his face in the shadows. I guess it's your call. What do you suggest we do?"

"Let me get back to you on this. Have your breakfast at the hotel and go on in to the Presidio to class. I know your days are pretty intense. Just give me a call later in the afternoon when you have some free time. By then I should be able to give you some advice."

"Thanks," responded Jenna and they hung up and followed Fred's suggestion.

⟊

It was a beautiful sunny afternoon. Marcus and Jenna were on break and outside the classroom. The particular building that their classroom was in was high enough on the Presidio grounds that they could see Monterey Bay.

"Look Jenna, there are not too many boats out there, but the slight breeze makes for a great day to sail. Look, there's the ketch. It's really a beautiful sight under full sail. Obviously, whatever we observed last night didn't inhibit its sailing capabilities." Then looking at his watch, Marcus said, "Jenna, you better call Fred. It's close to 2 o'clock our time which would mean it's close to quitting time for Fred. Let's see what he found out."

Jenna pulled out her cell and after the first ring Fred was on the line. "Hi Jenna, I've been waiting for your call. Look, if you are out of earshot of anybody put your phone on speaker so Marcus can hear also. First, the local FBI was pleased to hear about your find. Actually, they have been endeavoring to find out how drugs were getting into the country in your area. The local Mexican Mafia known as La eMe is very active in the prisons in that area and drugs coming in from Mexico have been showing up during these past summer months. How they have been getting in has been a mystery. Your sailboat scenario makes possible sense and they will be following up on it along with the Coast Guard. Your local contact should be Jose Rodriguez and I will text you his cell. Any information you should discover should be passed on to him. This is different from the contact I passed on to you earlier. Now, onto the incident that you experienced last night. There has been no report of any unidentified body being found in the marina area last night. So it can be assumed that whoever accosted you both and Jenna hit was removed from the scene either alive or dead. Further, this was probably accomplished by the local Mexican Mafia. They most certainly won't be present on Presidio grounds so you both are certainly safe there. When not there, you are on your own."

"How nice," responded Jenna. "Our bosses think we are vacationing in California going to language school not knowing that we are also possibly being pursued by both a New York Mafia organized-crime family and now the local Mexican Mafia. Isn't it nice to be popular."

"Jenna, don't be sarcastic. I recognize this is serious, and yes, you should inform the New York CIA office. Remember, you are CIA going to school; this an FBI affair, stay out of it."

Yohana sat on the deck of the family's 40-foot Newport ketch, sipping a coke, watching the setting sun. They had had a fun sail. Their crew, two girls from a local college, had been excused and her brother was down below finishing stowing the sails.

She was startled when her cell phone buzzed. It was stored in a small bag she kept tied to one of the cleats on deck. Retrieving it she was surprised to see a text message with three emojis: a sailboat, a set of eyes looking at it, and a skull and crossbones. It was from her dad and before she could respond, the phone rang.

"Dad, what's up?" She said as she answered the phone.

He immediately replied, saying, "Yohana, we have a problem. The other night our crew was observed unloading the boat. We always station someone in the parking lot as security and he caught them. They in turn immediately assaulted him when he approached them. He was almost killed. One of them hit him hard in the throat and he almost choked to death. It took a couple of days for him to recover. He told me it was a man and a woman. It was too dark to recognize their faces but the soft light of the full moon that night highlighted their hair. They were both blonde. Further, during the brief conversation that occurred before he was hit, he says he thought he heard a New York accent. I have no idea how he recognized that, but be that as it may, if they reported the activity, we could be in jeopardy. Further, if they haven't, they both should be eliminated if possible. Are you aware of anyone who would be watching our boat?"

"Not really," responded Yohana. "What should we do?"

"We will cease operations for now. I'll get word to Mexico. You and your brother should totally clean the boat. If authorities are alerted and come and inspect there should be no trace of cocaine on board. Keep me aware if anyone appears to take an interest in you or the boat." After those last words of her father, the phone went dead. Her brother appeared on deck and Yohana briefed him on what just happened.

"Yohana, it's been a few weeks now, but didn't you tell me that one of the patrons at the Sardine Factory was questioning you about our sailboat? You said you thought it was just a 'put on' to hit on you. Was he blond and was there a blond girl in that party?" asked Juan.

"You know he was, and yes, there was a blonde in the party," responded Yohana. "I haven't seen them down at the Marina, but I'm sure I'd recognize him if I saw him again. That party hasn't been back at the Sardine Factory either, at least not while I've been there. What are we supposed to do if you see them again? How do we know whether they were really the ones? Will Dad ask us to kill them?"

"I don't know, Yohana. This is getting a little scary. We could end up with our father, and I'm not too excited to go there."

CHAPTER 5

SAN FRANCISCO
EXCURSION

S hortly after the episode in the parking lot, coursework at the Presidio became pretty intense. Daily they were experiencing total immersion in either a half day of the classes or the full day. The whole class began to understand the *hanzi* and reading it appeared to become easier. However, understanding spoken Mandarin and speaking it themselves still appeared to be difficult.

LiJing praised the class for their capability and informed them that learning the *hanzi* would be extremely beneficial in the Far East as the characters were quite similar in all the Asian languages. The Japanese *kanji* is almost identical to the Chinese *hanzi*. Thus, understanding these characters should provide them the capability to read in many of the places in East Asia where they might be assigned. She indicated that the following day in class would be a field trip and that a van for the 10 of them would be at the bus parking lot in the morning in addition to the Presidio military bus. The trip into the city would be approximately two hours and they would be dropped off in Chinatown. They would have four hours to peruse the area and have lunch in one of the restaurants. When in that restaurant they should try to order in Mandarin. The following day in class they should be prepared to give a report on their accomplishments.

⊕

When the Wongs and Petersons arrived at the Transit Plaza, they were happy to see that right behind the military bus was a van. Boarding it with their other classmates, Sophia and Jenna sat together as did Jack and Marcus. Jenna began the conversation with Sophia as soon as they settled in.

"I'll tell you, Sophia, I am so excited about this trip. The last time I was in Chinatown in San Francisco was when I was out here looking at Berkeley as a possible college to go to. My mother and I had a great time touring the city, and Chinatown was one of the fun places we visited. It's going to be great to see if that restaurant we ate at is still there. I remember we had some great dim sum. I did go on the web and the restaurant called Great Eastern is supposed to have the greatest dim sum; in fact, they claim it was Obama's favorite restaurant when he was in San Francisco. We can certainly look at it as a possibility for lunch."

This was just the beginning of a chatty two hours between the couples on the way to the city. After almost exactly 2 hours, the van pulled up in front of Dragon's Gate on Grant Avenue and Bush Street, the entrance to Chinatown. The driver announced that this would also be the pickup place and all should be back there precisely at 3 PM. The two couples had decided that Jenna would be the tour guide since she had been there before. And they immediately started up Grant Avenue.

⊕

Nuncio Gambioni, though frustrated with his sister-in-law, stayed on his mission.

He changed his appearance by growing a beard and developed an entirely new hairstyle. Further, he found out California was no different than New York; money talks. Working with one of the room stewards of the Monterey Hotel, he was able to plant a bug in the Petersons' suite. Monitoring their conversations at home, he pretty much knew what they were going to do and where they would be. As such, he became aware of their field trip to San Francisco and decided that might be the place to stage an accident. So on the same morning that the Petersons left with their team, he too was on his way to the city. His thoughts: *Chinatown is really not that large. I know what they look like, and they probably wouldn't recognize me now. So I should be able to find them and we shall see; I might just be able to create a fatal accident.*

⊕

The team gathered for lunch at the Great Eastern. They straggled in in pairs with the Petersons and Wongs arriving at about 12:15 and the last ones arriving at 1:00. All tried their Mandarin when they ordered. They were surprised to see that the wait staff seemed to understand them. Jack Wong cornered one of the waiters and in Cantonese asked how come the staff understood Mandarin. He was told that due to the large Chinese tourist traffic, it became almost mandatory with the staff for some of them to learn Mandarin.

First in first out, the Wongs and Petersons were on their way out at about 1:30. As they left the restaurant, Jenna announced, "I think there's enough time," and looking at Marcus, she continued with, to get you on a cable car. That's really a must for anybody visiting the city for the first time."

"You think it's possible?" asked Jack.

"I'm sure. It's only a short walk up to Powell where we can catch the Powell Hyde cable car that goes down to Fisherman's Wharf and back. Come on, let's go," she said as she began to lead them up Sutter.

Sophia immediately said, "You three go on ahead. I'm in for shopping and there are some great stores right around here. I'll meet you back at the gate at three."

With that Marcus, Jenna and Jack started up Sutter to catch the cable car. They never would've dreamed that they were being followed and with the heavy foot traffic in downtown, it wouldn't be perceived at all. However, Nunzio Gambioni was close behind.

I bet they're going to take the cable car down to Fisherman's Wharf, he thought. *I'm going to gamble on that and speed across Union Square and catch it before it gets to Sutter. What a perfect place for an accident.*

As the car came up Powell from Union Square, it was pretty well occupied; the only room left was on the running boards. As they jumped on the left side of the car, Jenna said, "This is great. It's best to be on the outside. More fun and you can see a lot."

Just before they got to Jackson the conductor called out. "Hang on tight," and the car made a hard left turn.

"Look at all the people here," Marcus said excitedly.

"Yes, watching the cable car making a hard turn is somewhat of a sight so tourists tend to congregate and take pictures. Now in just a couple blocks it's going to turn right again to go down Hyde. Hang on."

As the car turned on Hyde, two arms from someone sitting shot out pushing Jenna and Marcus right off the car. The car was quickly brought to a stop and Nunzio was off and into the crowd.

⬤

Nunzio was out of breath as he got to the closest BART station. Pulling out his cell phone before going down the stairs, he made the call.

Adriana answered on the first ring and Nunzio said, "I pushed them both off a cable car when it was running. If they died or not, I have no idea. I'm on my way to the airport. I don't know if anybody saw me or what, but I'm out of here" With that he hung up his cell and ran down the stairs to catch the train.

⬤

The paramedic putting the last dressing on Jenna's knee said, "Are you sure you don't want to go to an ER. I can't force you and I admit nothing's broken and the surface wounds you both received should heal nicely. You both were damn lucky that there was a crowd there. Hitting a couple of people before the ground broke your fall. Luckily, they weren't hurt at all."

"No, we'll be fine," said Jenna and then with cow-like sweet eyes, she said, "You could do us a favor, though. Like instead of the ER, drop us off at Dragons Gate in Chinatown. We have a van picking us up to take us back to Monterey from there, and if we hurry we might just make it."

⬤

On the way back in the van, Sophia and Jenna were in deep conversation about the clothes that Sophia had bought while Marcus and Jack discussed the event that occurred.

"Do you remember who was sitting behind us on the cable car? Quite frankly, I have no idea. I never even looked. As soon as we jumped onboard my eyes were glued to the sites we were seeing as we traveled along. There were people there, I know, but I never looked at them."

"No, Marcus, I couldn't remember or describe anybody who was sitting on that car. But if it was that Mafia guy that's trying to kill you both, how would he know we were going to be in San Francisco?"

"That's a good question. We found out in class, came home on the bus together, went to dinner together, and I don't remember talking about it at all at dinner."

"You're right, Jack, neither do I. Jenna and I did chat before going to bed. The usual wife question, what am I going to wear? I wonder if our hotel room is bugged. I think I'm going to borrow some equipment from school and sweep the room. I'm sure they have the gear."

LiJing was pleasantly surprised the following day with the success her class had had in Chinatown. But both the class and LiJing could not believe the story that Marcus reported, concerning their attempted murder. Fortunately or unfortunately, this made the staff and students aware of Marcus and Jenna's situation, blowing their cover story that they were employed at the UN. Now all in the class knew that they were CIA agents with a Mafia mark on them.

LiJing reemphasized to the class that backgrounds and personal information of all students attending classes at the Presidio should be considered classified and most specifically what they just learned about the Petersons.

CHAPTER 6

QUESTIONABLE
FRIENDSHIP

It had been a tough week. The strain was obvious on Marcus and Jenna's faces and as the military bus pulled into the Transit Plaza, Marcus said, "Jenna, go home with Sophia and Jack. I'll walk over to Trader Joe's and pick up some snacks. Tell them it's cocktails at our place tonight. We need to babble away in English. This week of total immersion in Mandarin has been hell."

With that said, Marcus practically leapt off the bus and was on his way to Trader Joe's just a block away from the Transit Plaza. Walking in and heading over to the cheese area, he was startled to see Yohana there perusing the cheeses. His immediate thought was *do I approach her or try to avoid her. After that Sardine Factory meeting, I'm really not sure what to do.*

Before he could make a move, Yohana turned and recognizing him, smiled and walked over to greet him, saying, "I'm so sorry about the other night, but management is so strict at the Sardine Factory. That's a very important job for me so I wouldn't want to do anything that could jeopardize it. Look, my name is Yohana and I'd be happy to chat with you about sailing."

Before he could answer, Marcus's brain went into high speed. *Whew, I have got to be careful how I handle this. Befriending her would be good but I can't let on what we saw the other night or anything implying that I suspect her of being part of a smuggling organization. She is quite attractive; this should be easy.* With a big smile on his face, Marcus introduced himself and started a deep conversation about sailing. He related his racing days on Long Island sound and she described the racing in Monterey and how her ketch responded. The conversation ended with her inviting him and Jenna to sail with her and her brother on Saturday. With that they separated and went their separate ways shopping.

Marcus could not wait to get home and explain all this to Jenna. Little did he know that Yohana's main goal was to determine whether he and Jenna were the couple that accosted her father's people the other night in the marina parking lot.

⟐

Cocktail time at the Petersons was both relaxing and serious. They chatted among themselves, reflecting on the trip to San Francisco and the class activities for the week. However, on a more serious note, the invitation that Marcus had received from Yohana took the conversation into a planning and anticipation mode.

"Seriously," said Jack. "Are you sure you guys should go with Yohana and her brother? This could be a trap. You may not return."

"I really don't think so," said Marcus, "But there is a precaution we could take. I suggest that you two come down with us to the boat and see us off. That would pretty much tell them that if they did not return with us onboard there were witnesses who saw us leaving with them."

"That's pretty cool," said Jack. "That we can do. While you're away, I'll sweep both our apartments with that gear you brought home from the school to see if there're any bugs."

"Great plan, Jack. Here is the key to our place," said Marcus as he reached in his pocket for his keys.

Then Jack, looking at Jenna, asked, "Have you ever sailed in a small boat before?"

"Well, no and yes," she responded, "not in a sailboat, but my father used to love to go flounder fishing in City Island, a small town on Long Island Sound. He and one of his friends used to rent a rowboat and go out fishing. He took me along a couple times. We bounced around in the waves and it didn't seem to bother me. I guess riding the subways in New York sort of prepares you for that kind of motion."

"Well, sailing is a little bit different than bouncing around in a rowboat," said Marcus. "We will be gliding along at a pretty good speed and the only sound will be the hiss of the water on the hull and the wind in the sheets. I really look forward to it. It's one of my hobbies in the past that I really miss. There are really two types of sailing. There's just cruising when you're out on the water and just sailing about having a specific destination or just enjoying being out on the water. And then there is racing. Sailboat racing can be demanding, but it's fun and exciting. The boat, the sails, and the wind, are all you have to deal with in your effort to get from point A to point B faster than the other boats. You must know your boat's capabilities, how to handle its sails, and how to judge the wind."

"Well, after that description, I hope we're just going cruising," said Jenna.

⏀

Spirit was ready to sail. The jib was installed and raised but still furled as it was a roller reefing jib. The main and mizzen were installed and bundled on their respective booms, ready to be raised. Yohana, arranging the cushions in the cockpit, said to Juan as he came up from the cabin and entered the cockpit from the pilothouse, "Are we all set?"

"We're ready to go," said Juan, "I have a microphone on the binnacle in the cockpit and another in the main cabin. Both Bluetooth, they tie to a digital recorder down below. We will be able to record all conversation during the sail."

"Great. We can transfer the file to a flash drive and leave it in the dock locker. I'll tell Dad where it can be found. I'm sure the guy who was accosted in the parking lot the other night will be able to tell from the recording whether these are the people who were there. Oh, here they come. Big smile, Juan. Let's welcome them aboard."

Introductions were made as Marcus and Jenna got onboard, Jack released the deck lines and both Jack and Sophia waved as *Spirit* motored out of the harbor. Entering the bay Yohana put her into the wind and Juan pulled open the jib and started raising the main. Before Yohana or Juan could say a word, Marcus was up on deck and called out, "Yohana, I'll raise the mizzen" and proceeded to do so. Yohana, at the wheel, cut the engines and brought *Spirit* over onto a reach while Marcus and Juan trimmed the sails.

"Hey," called out Yohana, "You're quite comfortable sailing. No doubt you have done this before."

"I used to own a Lido 14 which I raced, but I also crewed on many large yachts in races. There's no question that after you've raced, there are things you do on deck unconsciously. That's what sailing is all about," responded Marcus.

"Would you like to take the wheel?" asked Yohana.

"Sure," responded Marcus as he immediately got up from where he was sitting and swapped places with Yohana. Getting behind the binnacle and grabbing hold of the wheel, he said, "Where are we heading?"

"Try to maintain this course. We're heading toward Santa Cruz, not that we're going that far, but it heads us toward the middle of the bay. Also try to keep her on a close reach, she runs well there. You can often get seven knots. If the wind shifts, we may have to tack or put her on more of a beam reach. We should maintain this course until we get to the middle of the bay. If the wind stays when we get there, you can slack off to a starboard broad beam reach. That should head us toward the bay entrance and we will level out a bit and maybe then have lunch. The Sardine Factory packed us a great lunch, which they usually do. One of the perks of the job."

On the current run the heel was roughly 20 degrees and Marcus looked over at Jenna and saw a scared expression and hands firmly holding the cockpit rail. Juan stood up heading into the pilothouse, asking, "Beer, water or Sprite?"

"Beer, Juan, thanks," said Marcus, then looking at Jenna said, "Jenna, try to relax and enjoy. We are not going to tip over. This is normal when sailing. Soon we will be on a different course and the boat will level out more. Enjoy."

"I'll have a beer also, Juan," said Yohana as she stood up and shed her sweats, revealing a very brief bikini and saying, "It's delightful in the sun. Time for a little tan. I normally can't do this as I do most of the sailing. It's great having another sailor onboard. Oh, Juan sails but he really doesn't like to. We have an agreement about sailing. I skipper, he handles the sails."

With a facial expression changing from fright to total annoyance, Jenna said, "I'll have water, please, Juan." and then looking at Yohana, she thought, *She is a tramp. Stripping down to a bikini and cozying up next to Marcus. I thought this was a sailing trip, not a watch-me-steal-your-husband game.*

⟨⊕⟩

As they came in sight of Santa Cruz, Yohana, who had been lying on the forward deck getting her tan, got up and came back to the cockpit and started barking orders.

"Marcus, I'll take the helm and bring her about. We will be heading towards the tip of the Monterey Peninsula and with this wind I think we can make a spinnaker run. Should be fun. You will have to help Juan with the spinnaker. We will be furling the jib and raising the spinnaker and putting the spinnaker pole on the starboard side. Jenna, keep your head down. When I bring her about both the main and the mizzen booms will be swinging over to port."

A lot happened in a short period of time and Jenna just hung on tight with eyes the size of an owl watching what was going on all around her. With the wind at their back, the sails, main and mizzen out to the port side and spinnaker ahead and filled, *Spirit* picked up speed. "Amazing," yelled Marcus as he climbed back into the cockpit. "I didn't think a Newporter could carry a Spinnaker."

"Well, it's a little tricky," replied Yohana, "I had the spinnaker made special. With this wind we should really pick up speed. It will almost feel like we are up on plane. Come, Marcus, you can have the helm back. In the far distance you should be able to see the aquarium. Try to maintain a course in that general direction. However, watch the wind and keep all sheets full."

Yohana's main goal was to keep Marcus as close to the binnacle as possible to record his voice. The fact that he obviously loved sailing made this easy and that he appeared to be attracted to her made the whole operation fun.

Juan went down the forward hatch after setting the spinnaker and now came out of the pilothouse saying, "Are we all ready for lunch?" and then looking at Jenna said, "Come below with me. *Spirit* will be pretty level on this run. You can give me a hand with lunch and see the roomy cabin we have below. A Newporter is pretty comfy for a sailboat."

His obvious goal was to record her voice on the microphone he had hidden below. She followed him and was surprised to see how expansive below deck was with the pilothouse and the main cabin. In the tour he pointed out the door to the toilet saying, "The pot is in there should you need it. Onboard it's called the head."

Jenna didn't comment but she was surprised to see a *hanzi* character for toilet on the door. She was also surprised to see how many electronics were down below. What caught her eye initially was the GPS screen, pinpointing exactly where they were. They continued to chat away as they unpacked the lunch that had been provided by the Sardine Factory. Juan prompted the small talk to keep the conversation going. Primary goal: keep talking and record the voice.

Meanwhile, Yohana had positioned herself again forward tending the spinnaker sheet and soaking up the sun. Glancing back towards the stern, she couldn't tell whether Marcus was looking at her or just looking forward navigating *Spirit.*

He may be married to Jenna but I think he's attracted to me, she thought. *He is good-looking and certainly knows how to sail. I almost hope he isn't identified as the possible adversary of my father's team. Knowing my father's men, if they are identified as the culprits that observed the drug unloading the other night, in a short time they will be taken out. Not so sure that's a good thing. It could reflect back on Juan and me. Hmm hmm hmm, maybe the recording could get damaged.*

Jenna and Juan emerged from the pilothouse and laid a fabulous spread in the cockpit. Yohana, on the forward deck, picked up her towel and came back to the cockpit, saying, "Marcus, I'll take the helm. Sit down, eat and enjoy."

Spirit had leveled out and, running with a spinnaker, they were going along at a good clip. Suddenly they were joined by a flock of birds and a small pod of Pacific White-Sided Dolphin. Jenna remarked, "We've got company. They look like dolphins but I've never seen any with white sides."

"Probably not," said Yohana, "They are called Pacific white-sided dolphin and are quite common out here. In fact, Monterey Bay is known for dolphins and porpoises. They run tour boats out of Fisherman's Wharf just to see them."

Other than the dolphin visit, the rest of the sail was quite calm. Juan and Yohana did their best to keep the conversation going during the rest of the sail, obviously hoping to get as much recorded as possible.

⟨⟨⟩

They dropped the spinnaker as they approached Monterey, and as Marcus and Juan stowed the sails, Yohana started the engine and slowly guided *Spirit* into the marina. Jenna pulled her cell phone out and made a quick call to Jack, letting him know that they were on their way back.

"I hope you've enjoyed the sail," said Yohana to Jenna. "That last leg into Monterey was really a joy. Sailing with the wind is always fun."

"It was great, Yohana. I have to admit I had a little trepidation about coming but it turned out to be a real pleasure. That dolphin visit that we experienced made it fantastic. Thanks so much. Oh, and the lunch was outstanding."

Then turning to Marcus as he climbed back into the cockpit, Yohana said, "You're a great sailor, Marcus. I may call on you to crew on some of the competitive regattas we have."

"I'd be happy to," responded Marcus.

As they pulled into their slip in the marina, Jack was there and helped them tie up. In a matter of minutes, goodbyes and thank yous were exchanged and Marcus and Jenna were in the car with Jack for the brief ride back to the hotel. "You both look like you got a little sun, so I suggest a little aloe lotion tonight. How was the sail?"

"Oh, it was great. That sure is a beautiful little yacht," said Marcus "Newporters are known for being quite comfortable but due to their beam not particularly a racing sailboat. I was really surprised how well she performed. And they treated us to a great lunch on the trip. All in all it was a lot of fun. Oh, we were also visited by a pod of dolphin which made it quite exciting."

"Talk about room," said Jenna, "I couldn't believe what was below deck. I was surprised to see how many instruments they had in the pilothouse, which included a full-screen GPS. You could see where we were all the time. I also spotted an unusual thing down below. The head had a Mandarin *hanzi* character on its door that means toilet. Maybe the yacht was owned by the Chinese at one time. Certainly, the Mexican Mafia would not have put it there. I was going to ask Juan about it but it just slipped my mind in the hustle of getting lunch. Incidentally, Yohana let Marcus do just about all the sailing. She stripped down to her bikini and laid on a towel on the forward deck in full view of Marcus as he was steering the yacht. I think he was smitten a bit."

"Well, she is an attractive girl," responded Marcus with a somewhat sheepish grin. Then quickly changing the subject, he said, "Jack, did you get a chance to sweep the apartments?"

"Oh, did I. You wouldn't believe. There were two bugs in your place and one in ours. I contacted the manager and showed her what we found. It really caught her off guard. She was embarrassed and upset, informing us that the staff that serviced the hotel was longstanding and reliable. Later in the afternoon she got back to us and indicated that upon questioning, one of the women admitted to accepting money from someone to allow them to go into the apartments. They claimed that they had forgotten their key. Needless to say, she's been fired."

"Well, after their attempt to take us out in San Francisco, whoever they are may have fled the scene. However, if they're still here, they are no longer going to be getting information on us. It was good we found the bugs, but it still doesn't give us total peace of mind," responded Marcus. "I'm afraid we have to continue to keep our guard up."

⟨D⟩

The next morning Yohana's cell phone woke her up. "Dad, so early in the morning. What's going on?"

"My people got the recording that you left in the chest on the pier. They said the conversation was somewhat muddled and too many people were talking at the same time. Therefore, they couldn't really determine any specific voice. The one that was accosted didn't recognize any voice on the recording at all. So we really can't tell whether your so-called friends were the adversaries in the parking lot. You might try taking them for a sail again. Since nothing really happened; nobody came to inspect our boat. It could've been tourists and they probably have left town. However, I've got another issue. We will be getting another human cargo. It's good you had to clean the ship. I will give you the details in a few days. When I call, please be prepared to give me dates of scheduled regattas. Also, I believe they will want them offloaded in Santa Cruz. I suggest you or Juan go up there and check out the marinas, look for a good place to offload."

"But Dad." Before she could say anything else, the phone went dead. Typical for prison calls.

◑

The days seemed to fly by in the late summer. Heavy class work during the week and partying on the weekend when time permitted kept the Wongs and Petersons totally occupied. They did manage to get to the aquarium and Jenna's uncle Mark gave them a fantastic tour, taking them behind the scenes and showing them all that was involved in running such a facility.

Yohana did call on Marcus to crew with her in one of the competitive regattas. They came in second in their class, which Marcus thought was great considering it was a Newporter cruising yacht rather than a racing sailboat.

At Marcus's suggestion, Yohana invited the Wongs, Marcus, and Jenna out for an afternoon sail as sort of a thank you for allowing Marcus to crew. Sofia declined, saying if she was ever going on the water, it better be in a big ship that doesn't roll with the sea, as she always had struggled with motion sickness.

CHAPTER 7

A QUESTIONABLE
ASSIGNMENT

I t had been an intensive week at the Presidio. The Petersons and the
Wongs were looking forward to a break on the weekend. The sun was
still high in the sky and the walk down to Cannery Row was to be savored
in the warm environment.

"Let's eat at Schooners Coastal Kitchen at the Monterey Plaza Hotel. We haven't been there in a while and it will be a great place to plan
our weekend," said Jenna. "A bowl of their cioppino and a bottle or two
of wine will relax us and get us in the planning mood, I'm sure." Settling
in at a window table, ordering their meal and toasting the wine, the planning began.

"How about a run and picnic on Monterey municipal beach tomorrow," suggested Marcus.

"I'd like to spend the day wandering around Carmel," said Sophia.
"We could do that on Sunday," chimed in Jenna. And with dinner and
copious quantities of wine, the evening went quite late with their

planning as well as their review of their activities during the week. They struggled back to their lodgings after the coastal kitchen closed. They mutually agreed that a "sleep-in" was necessary so they would meet for breakfast at 10.

⊕

Jenna woke with a start. She wasn't sure which woke her up first, Marcus's snoring or her cell phone sitting on the bedside table.

Looking at the clock, she commented to herself, *Who would be calling us at five in the morning.* Crawling over Marcus, who was still sound asleep, she grabbed her cell phone. Marcus never woke up; he just rolled over and began snoring again. Looking at the screen and seeing the call was coming from CIA office in New York, she quickly put the phone to her ear and in a somewhat groggy voice answered, "Hello, Jenna Peterson here." After listening for a few minutes, she sat up straight, very alert, and answered, "Yes, sir, tomorrow at noon. Yes, we will be there". Closing the phone and shaking Marcus awake, she said, "Good morning, dear, happy Saturday, we have got a little issue today."

Rubbing his eyes, Marcus said, "Jenna, what's going on. It's still dark." Then looking at the clock on the side table, he said, "It's five in the morning. What's the problem? Was that your cell phone I heard earlier, with its crazy ringtone?"

"Yes, that was our boss on the phone. The big boss, the New York Station Chief. They will be arriving at the Monterey airport at 12 noon on the Gulfstream G650 and we are to be there."

"What's this all about?"

"He didn't say. He just said, 'be there.' Oh, and he said the local FBI head will be there also. He didn't say his name so I don't know whether that would be Jose Rodriguez or not."

"OMG, we have to tell the Wongs. That pretty much shoots our plans for the weekend. Are we going anywhere or just meeting him?" said Marcus.

"I have no idea. I'm sure we'll find out when we get there. Oh, he did say that we would be meeting on the Gulfstream."

⊕

The electric cart taking them from the terminal down to the general aviation area where the Gulfstream was parked moved along at its top speed. Jenna and Marcus had been totally surprised when they had entered the terminal building. Someone immediately approached them, mentioning their names, showing his security badge and instructing them to follow him. Before they knew it, they were seated on the back bench of the cart and on their way.

"Marcus, I've never been on the Gulfstream. When you arrived home from London on your last mission in it, I was surprised how large it is. What's it like inside? Is it big enough for a meeting?" asked Jenna as they rode along.

"It's quite luxurious," said Marcus. "It was originally owned by a drug lord and confiscated by the CIA on a raid. No cost to the taxpayers. And yes, it can hold a small meeting quite comfortably; you will see."

As the car approached the plane, Marcus was quite surprised to see the same attractive flight attendant who had been on it when he flew back from England and was surprised to hear her call out, "Welcome aboard, Marcus. I missed you."

Jenna didn't appreciate that welcome and, looking at Marcus as he got out of the cart, she said, "What was that all about?"

"Oh, nothing," said Marcus. "She took care of Brady and me on the trip home and she was quite comforting. Remember, we were pretty shook up."

Upon boarding they were immediately ushered to the lounge area of the Gulfstream. It normally provides seating for four, but some folding chairs had been added. They were surprised to see local FBI Agent José Rodriguez along with their boss and New York CIA Station Chief Alonzo. "Please be seated," he said. "I believe we are all here and we can proceed.

"You both are about to get an additional assignment. It will not interrupt your current program at the Presidio. In fact, it may be enhanced by that, and yes, your instructor and commanding officer LiJing Chen has been informed. But first let me give you a small background briefing. You both are well aware of the China threat and our concerns about spying, technology transfer, and the whole gamut that's going on. You may not be aware that the current administration, in an effort to mitigate this, has frozen all visas from China. Sadly, intelligence is indicating that certain large companies and universities are involved with smuggling Chinese technical personnel into the country, their belief being these highly technical personnel are better and cheaper than what can be recruited in-country. They obviously appear to be overlooking the fact that these personnel provide a conduit to flow our technical advancements from both industry and university research back to China. This has to be curtailed."

"I understand all this," said Marcus. "We are well aware of what you just said based on our periodic security briefings. How do we fit into the mitigation process?"

"The FBI and we have been working together on this effort for some time. Your local FBI contact, Agent Rodriguez, apprised us of your discovery and suspicion of drugs being smuggled into Monterey via a sailboat. Agent Rodriguez followed up on your suspicions and determined that was true but no action was taken."

With a concerned expression on her face, Jenna interrupted the conversation, saying, "Rodriguez, you never told us. Why?"

With a stern expression, Station Chief Alonzo looked at Jenna, saying, "That is not of concern right now. Listen up. We suspect that this operation may be or already has been utilized to smuggle undocumented Chinese into the country and into a university and tech industry here on the West Coast. Our concern is not so much the Mexican Mafia that is conducting this, but who are they accomplishing this for, and who is paying for it."

"I am not surprised," responded Marcus. He then related the friendship they had established with Yohana and her brother and further what they discovered when they sailed with them.

"Other than your discovery of the drugs being unloaded and the altercation you had, have you developed any idea on when a smuggling operation is scheduled for Yohana and her sailboat?" asked Station Chief Alonzo.

"We can't predict that in advance. But I pretty much can tell when it's about to happen," responded Marcus. "As you are aware, Monterey Bay is a magical experience for sailors and as such, many regattas are scheduled during the summer season. During those regattas, which we enjoy watching, I became aware that the local Coast Guard tends to stay in port and more or less assists in conducting the regattas. They do this primarily by keeping their two local ships in the bay and curtailing non-racing boats entering the racing course. What we have also observed is that Yohana most always enters *Spirit* in these regattas. She is a competitive sailor and has outfitted her Newporter for racing. During certain regattas that we have watched, the Newporter does not return with the rest of the competitive sailboats to the marina. We suspect that she leaves the bay for the ocean when not returning. There is usually considerable boat traffic in and out of the bay during race days and her departure would not be noticed. I would guess that that would be when *Spirit* would be picking up a smuggled load, personnel or drugs. They probably return later at night as in most cases, the next day when we go for breakfast at Fisherman's Wharf, *Spirit* is docked."

"It's probably apparent, I love to sail. As such we have tried to develop a relationship with Yohana to go sailing. Jenna and I have sailed with her twice, once by ourselves and once we brought our classmate Jack Wong along. In addition, I did crew for her in one of the regattas. Needless to say, in that regatta we returned to the marina with the rest of the boats."

"We have been tracking a similar operation up in the Seattle area but have not yet been able to crack the operation. I think what we suspect is going on here is a somewhat smaller smuggling process that might be easier to crack and fully determine the enterprising organizations accomplishing it," said Station Chief Alonzo. "That brings us to your assignment. I want you to go undercover and really befriend Yohana. Try to participate in the operation, gathering the intelligence we need for further prosecution."

During this discussion Jenna's face changed. It began to show real concern. She didn't have to say a word but all in the room could sense she was not at all happy. On the other hand, Marcus perked up and with a large smile responded, "That shouldn't be a problem. I think we have become quite close due to my sailing ability."

With that said, Station Chief Alonzo stood and said, "I think we're adjourned here now."

⊕

They were no sooner in their car driving back to the hotel than Jenna's fears and jealousy erupted. Turning to Marcus, she said, "And what do you think Station Chief Alonzo meant by befriending her? Remember, we are married. At least I thought so. Are you supposed to sleep with her? How far do you go with this undercover bit?"

"Jenna, stop that," responded Marcus. "What he's asking is for me to gain her friendship and respect such that she invites me to participate in the operation when it should occur. Nothing more. He didn't say or imply anything about an emotional involvement. Jenna, we are CIA agents. Part of our job at times is becoming friends with the adversaries to gather our intelligence. Get off your jealous kick. I love you and you know that. Let's focus on our assignment; we are a team, remember. Now, one of the things I think we should do is join the Monterey Peninsula Yacht Club. I did do a little research the other day and you don't have to be a boat owner to join, you just have to like sailing. They run all the regattas and Yohana is a member. They have a lot of social events so joining it could be fun and also a possible source to find out more about Yohana."

After that bit of dialogue, the car went silent and as they drove the rest of the way home, Marcus's mind went into overdrive. *This assignment is going to be quite a challenge regardless of what I just told Jenna. I really don't know how to do this. We still don't know the relationship with the Mexican Mafia drug runners that are using her boat or her involvement. And who knows after our encounter with them in the parking lot, they could be still after us. Getting close to Yohana not only involves gaining her trust but me trusting her. And yes, she's not hard to look at and appears to be quite personable. Developing a friendship but avoiding the physical and emotional relationship will not be easy.*

Jenna was also in deep thought. *I believe what he says, but is this going to be another Martina? She tracked him on our last two assignments and I'm sure seduced him somewhere along the way. I'm sure if she were still alive she would be tracking him today. The way Yohana was looking at him on the sailing trip, I'm sure she has similar thoughts.*

CHAPTER 8

REVELATION

After the briefing they connected back up with the Wongs, continu-ing their planned weekend activities and since the Wongs had been involved with everything that happened since their arrival, they had to be briefed on Marcus's new assignment. At dinner that night Marcus briefed them and opened the suggestion of joining the yacht club.

Not really surprised, Jack Wong immediately sided with Marcus, saying, "Hey, I'd love to join the yacht club with you. I haven't done much sailing but I did sail a few times in Lake Michigan and certainly had a great time when we went out with Yohana."

Sofia immediately chimed in, saying, "No way, I'm not into sailing at all, you know that."

"Hold on, Sophia," said Marcus, "I did some research, and the club-house is excellent. They have a restaurant, and bar that's open all the time. In addition, they have many social events. It could be a great place to hang out as opposed to us wandering around to all the restaurants in town. You don't have to own a boat to join. You don't have to be into racing. They have a group that gets together monthly just talking about cruising. Further, as members we have the opportunity to go to yacht clubs all over the world as most all yacht clubs have reciprocity. It could be great and dues are not that steep. You have to be sponsored by a member to join but I found out that can be arranged. After the briefing I immediately emailed LiJing to find out if she knew anybody in the yacht club and was surprised to find out she is a member and could handle getting us sponsored without a problem. She doesn't own a boat either but joined just for the social aspects. In this town socially, if you're a golfer, you join a country club and if you're a sailor, you join the yacht club. It's that simple.

At this point Jack stood up, raising a glass, saying, "Here's to our new adventure."

⟨D⟩

It happened so fast. In less than two weeks, the Petersons and Wongs were attending the Friday night "New Members Night and Wine Tasting." Marcus was extremely happy that new members night included wine tasting. Here local vineyards came and presented selections from their wineries.

They were seated with LiJing chatting about the wine when much to Jenna's surprise, Mark and Susan Jones arrived at their table and sat down. "Uncle Mark, I had no idea you were into the sailing," said Jenna.

"We are really not, but working at the Aquarium and living in Salinas, it became obvious that politically it was wise to be engaged socially in Monterey, thus yacht club membership. But it's really great. There are a lot of activities here that we enjoy and I'm sure you will too," responded Mark.

Conversation around the table was primarily about the wine and LiJing briefing them on all the activities that she participated in. As the conversation continued, Marcus's eyes were roving around the room more or less scanning the membership and then he spotted Yohana and Juan at the bar. Seeing her, he immediately injected into the conversation, "LiJing, what's the story on the Mendezes?"

LiJing turned to Marcus with a somewhat surprised look, saying, "That's an interesting one. Let me explain. Much occurred before I even arrived in Monterey or joined the club but I learned much from past club members. It appears the club is more or less their second home. Growing up, they both participated in our youth group learning to sail. Their father bought them Sabots and as they matured, they continued to participate in activities in the club, all funded by their father. The Mendezes were members of the yacht club but never participated. It was primarily for their children. In fact. members say they had no idea in those days what their parents did. They had a modest house over in the Latino section of Monterey and the father was out of town most of the time. Like many of the members' children, they hung out at the clubhouse. In fact, we have a teenage room upstairs. In their high school years, their father bought them a Star boat. I don't know if you're familiar with it, but that is a popular racing sloop and we have several of them in the club. They became quite good at racing. Yohana being the older of the two more or less became the skipper of the team and they won many regattas. They both went to junior college here and supposedly as a combined graduation present, he bought them the Newporter. That really didn't go over too well with Yohana as it's more or less a cruising sailboat as opposed to a racer. That occurred about when I joined the club. Then came the big revelation: the source of income. There was a big raid by the feds on a Mexican Mafia organization in the area and it turned out her father headed it. He is in prison now. The club didn't want to punish the kids for their father's crimes, so they more or less granted them permanent membership. And I'm sure you're aware that *Spirit* doesn't have a permanent slip but is tied up just outside the club's permanent slips alongside the last finger. Club members arranged a job for Juan as a caddie at Pebble Beach and Yohana works at the Sardine Factory. I'm not sure whether the mother is employed or not, but with all that in place, they seem to have the finances to pay their dues here and to live a good life, and sail."

At about that time Yohana and Juan came over to their table, Yohana saying, "Marcus, I'm so glad you joined the club. Please sign up with the crew moderator. That way you'll be official if you crew for me in any of the regattas. Welcome aboard." And with that said, they both were off.

"Well, Marcus, looks like your assignment is officially launched," said LiJing.

◍

The corporate board room of Avocado Corporation, the largest tech giant in the US, contained three people: the CEO, the COO, and the Managing Director of their operation in China.

The latter had the floor, saying, "Look, our operation in China almost mirrors what you have here in Silicon Valley. And without it we could not manage our marketing and manufacturing capability that resides over there and provides over 50% of our sales. Further, cycling personnel from our facility there through our facility here maintains an economical workforce, providing total capability in both countries. Now that the government has banned all visas for people coming from China, we must use alternate means to keep the personnel float in operation, even if that is somewhat illegal. I know the government is accusing China of stealing our intellectual property and thus the ban on Chinese visas. Whether that is true within our operation, I have no idea. There is no way we have the capability of determining which of our employees are tied to the Communist Party, the government, or the military there. If we tried, it could jeopardize everything we have going in that country."

A disturbed look appeared in the CEO's face as he said, "Doing business with a Mexican cartel and a California Mexican Mafia is not my idea of an acceptable alternate means."

"I'm afraid the activity has already been initiated and at this time there is no way to cancel," responded the COO.

"I understand some universities are employing the same process with graduate students from China. I want legal advised of this operation," said the CEO "If the government found out about this, I have no idea what the ramifications would be."

CHAPTER 9

THE SURPRISE CAPTURE

It was a warm night and the Wongs and Petersons had just finished a pleasurable meal at Fish Hopper's restaurant on Cannery Row.

"Meals at the yacht club are all right but it's really most enjoyable to have a good meal at Cannery Row," said Sofia.

"You got that right," said Jenna.

"It's such a beautiful evening, Jenna, let's walk home," said Marcus. And then turning, said, "Jack, if it's okay with you, Jenna and I will take the coastal trail back to Fishermen's Wharf and home."

"Not a problem. Go ahead. We'll drive back to the hotel. See you in the morning," responded Jack. As the Wongs walked up to the parking lot where they left the car, the Petersons started down the trail.

"With the full moon tonight, I think it's bright enough where there are no streetlights. We should have no problem walking, but I have my mini flashlight in my purse," said Jenna. "If necessary, we can use that."

"Great," said Marcus. "Let's go." Hand in hand they started on the trail. They were not alone as there were several others walking along the coastal trail but as they left the Cannery Row area, the trail became less populated. It winds a bit along the coast towards Fisherman's Wharf and goes through several areas where there are large trees, thus shielding the moonlight.

They were totally unaware that four people in dark clothing were following them just a few paces back. They had just rounded a bend in a tree-lined area somewhat below the Presidio's north gate when in a matter of seconds, the four were upon them. It was like an orchestrated maneuver. Simultaneously, two adversaries attacked each one of them, one grabbing from behind and the other thrusting a rag filled with chloroform in their face. Their initial struggling only lasted seconds when they collapsed to the ground.

⟪⟫

Just below the Presidio Museum outside the north gate stood the old Presidio stable, probably one of the last of the original buildings and currently used by the grounds staff for storage of equipment and supplies used to maintain the grounds. At this time of night this section of the Presidio grounds was totally deserted and it was surprising to see a van parked at one end of the stable and lights emanating from just inside one end of the building.

⟪⟫

Marcus slowly came to consciousness and immediately realized there was tape over his mouth and his hands were bound behind him with zip ties. He was lying on a musty floor and the smell of fertilizer was causing him almost to choke. Something was pulling his hands up and down and his mind came to full consciousness. *We were obviously drugged and taken somewhere. Could that be Jenna behind me,* Marcus thought.

"Murn murn murn murn," came through the tape as Marcus tried to speak.

Moving his hands up and down, he heard, "Murn murn murn murn" in a slightly higher pitch. *I knew it, he thought, that's got to be Jenna. We're tied together in some sort of a garden building.* His eyes began to get used to the darkness and the faint light from the moon streaking through the cracks of the old wooden siding provided enough light to see his surroundings. *Whoa, we are pretty close to burlap bags of groundcover, fertilizer, or whatever. Think I see some sort of machinery little further away.* Moving his jaw, his lips and his tongue, he was finally able to move the tape a bit that was over his mouth. With a little effort he was able to get his face close to the burlap bags and started to rub his mouth back and forth on the bag. The tape finally caught and he was able to pull it off from his face to the bag.

"Jenna," he said. "I was able to get the tape off my mouth on this burlap bag. If I can wiggle you over here close, you should be able to do the same and we can talk." Together they squiggled around and got Jenna's face close to the burlap bags and she started doing what Marcus had done, to try and get the tape off her mouth. While this was going on, Marcus became aware of faint voices somewhere in the building. *That's Italian I'm hearing. I bet Nunzio and Adriano are behind this,* he thought.

"Jenna, when you get the tape off, don't speak loud, our adversaries are here, I can hear them talking," he said softly. "From the volume of their voices, it appears they may be at the other end of the building and it sounds like they're speaking Italian. If so, it could be Adriana and Nunzio. I'm sure they are planning our demise. I think we are in the old Presidio's stable that's by the Presidio museum. I believe we visited it when we first toured Monterey. As I recall, it's just a bunch of box stalls filled with landscaping equipment. We've got to try to escape."

"I hear you," said Jenna in a soft voice.

"Oh, good, you were able to get the tape off. While you were working on the tape on your mouth, I could see across the stall some sort of garden machinery. If we can work our way over there we might be able to find something sharp to rub our hands over and cut the zip ties that are tying us together."

⟨⊕⟩

The end box stall of the Presidio stable had been converted into somewhat of an office. Two two-drawer file cabinets and a 2 X 8 sheet of plywood formed a desk on one wall with an old wooden office chair. A straight-back chair and a six-foot bench surrounding a large crate filled out the area.

Nunzio Gambioni sat in the office chair; Adriana Gambioni sat in the straight-back chair. Two other crime family members sat on the bench. The large crate held four Starbucks coffee cups. Nunzio was saying, "We should be able to catch the noon flight tomorrow back to New York. The basic plan is working better than I thought. I had anticipated getting Marcus and Jenna sometime this weekend but following them and seeing them take the trail just worked to our advantage. Now that we have them bound and gagged in the back stall so they can't go anywhere, I suggest we go get something to eat. High tide doesn't occur until 2:00 AM in the morning. At that time we will come back, chloroform them again, take off the zip ties and take them out and throw them in the drink at the very place we grabbed them on the trail. Hopefully they will experience a tragic accidental drowning death in the surf."

As Nunzio was saying this, Adriana's face lit up and raising her coffee up, she said, "Justice at last. They had to pay for Angelina and Franco's deaths."

"There's an all-night pub downtown. It's probably less than a 10 minute run from here. Everyone in the SUV, let's go," said Nunzio.

⟨Ⅾ⟩

Jenna and Marcus were inching their bodies toward the other side of the stall where Marcus thought he saw the gardening equipment. As they inched their way along, they paused as they heard the sound of a car.

"Jenna, did you hear that? I think somebody's driving away," said Marcus, "Whether that's one or all of our captors I don't know but let's try to move a little faster. We've got to get out of here."

"Marcus, this isn't working. We are hardly moving. We are moving our bodies but we don't seem to be making that much progress towards the other side of the stall."

"Jenna, we've got to keep trying. It's our only hope." Just then they heard another car noise.

"Marcus, that's a car. It sounds like it's right outside. OMG, they're back."

"Jenna, listen. It sounds like another car is also out there." Two car doors slammed and then a loud call.

"Marcus, are you here?"

"Jenna, that sounds like Rodriguez."

"Yes, Jose," yelled Marcus, "We're here." The stall door opened and in walked José Rodriguez and another FBI agent with flashlights.

"Thank God," yelled Jenna.

As the zip ties were cut and Marcus and Jenna were helped to stand up, Marcus said, "How did you find us?"

"You must have your cell phone on you somewhere, because that's what we tracked. We were alerted by the FBI in New York that they suspected that the Gambionis were coming out here for another try at hitting you both. When we got that word, we started tracking your cell. That was about two days ago. So we knew where you were all the time. On a hunch, we tracked the car rentals at SFO and a day ago got lucky. We were alerted that the Gambionis had rented an SUV from Hertz. We've been tracking them ever since. We did not alert you as our game plan was to catch them in the operation. You can't arrest anybody for visiting Monterey but you certainly can for attempted murder. We felt by tracking you both any attempt that was made we would be there in time to save you."

As José was relating the story, you could see the fire in Marcus's eyes as he listened and as Jose finished, it erupted with Marcus screaming, "Holy shit, both of us could've been killed. Pretty gutty playing with our lives. Don't get me wrong, we are happy to be saved but I'm not excited about being used as bait".

"Well, I don't blame you," said Jose, "You have a right to be pissed off. The agent we had following the SUV saw them park down at Cannery Row and thought they were just going to dinner, so he didn't bother worrying about them anymore. The agent at the office that was tracking you saw you go to dinner at Cannery Row and just assumed it was your normal evening, so he didn't pay much attention to it either. No one was too concerned until we got a call from Jack Wong. When you didn't show up at the hotel, he immediately called us. That put us in action. I was alerted and based on your cell location, immediately came here to find you. A call went out on the SUV and we were alerted that it was parked at the all-night pub in old town. Just before we pulled into the parking lot here, I got a text that the Gambioni crew was arrested at the pub."

"I have to admit neither Jenna nor I ever saw who actually grabbed us. But I do remember hearing Nuncio's voice just before I was slapped with a rag of chloroform. Later, when we woke up in the Presidio stable we heard Italian being spoken somewhere at the other end of the building. Whether that was Nunzio or not would be hard to say," responded Marcus.

"I wouldn't concern myself about that, Marcus. In fact, I would just forget about what all happened. You won't have to testify and with four of them, it will be no problem getting a confession. Just consider that issue is no longer a problem and get back to working your main assignment. Put the Gambioni family vendetta behind you. Come, hop in my car. I'll run you back to your hotel."

Nunzio and Adriana and their two associates sat in a booth close to the window of the all-night pub. They had just ordered their breakfast when Nunzio, spotting two local police cars pulling into the lot, quickly said, "I think we may have an issue. Adriana, quick, go to the restroom and don't come out until you get a text from me."

CHAPTER 10

THE GREAT ESCAPE

LiJing surprised the class by arriving slightly late wearing a typical Chinese dress and greeted them all in Mandarin. She proceeded to explain to the class that today would be the first of their three escape room journeys that she had apprised them of at the beginning of the program. Then in English she said, "You will be divided into your original assigned teams and placed in the escape rooms. By the way, how many of you are aware of escape rooms? I mentioned them at the beginning of our program and nobody asked me about them then so I assumed all knew what they were."

Most hands went up but some did not. So she continued in English, saying, "Escape rooms can be 1, 2, or 3 interconnecting rooms and once you are in them you will try to find the key to the exit door which may be the door you entered or the door at the other end of the complex. There are series of puzzles to be solved that lead you to where the key exists. In addition, the key may be an actual key or it could be a series of numbers or letters required to open a combination lock. We have set up what we call the Hutong area where we have two Siheyuan dwellings each with three interconnecting rooms. They are representative of what you would find in the Hutong area in Beijing. All written clues and instructions in the rooms will be in *hanzi* and you are to conduct all conversation with your team members in Mandarin. In the course of executing your escape, if English is heard, five minutes will be added to your escape time. The area is set up in a warehouse at the other end of the base and a minibus is just outside the class building waiting for you. Please all board the bus now."

⟨⟩

On the drive over to the escape room the Petersons and the Wongs chatted about the coming event. Jenna said, "You know, Marcus, Jack and my team are going to win."

"Where would you get that idea," responded Marcus. Jack Wong had a grin on his face while Sophia just rolled her eyes.

Jenna continued, "We have a secret weapon and if you think about it, you might figure it out."

Picking up on the conversation, Jack immediately said, "Marcus, I think Jenna may have a point. Maybe a wager is in order?"

Sophia quickly said, "Don't involve me."

Jack said with a smile, "No, it's just between Marcus and Jenna. Somehow Jenna thinks our team has an advantage over yours but that might not be true."

Marcus quickly picked up on the idea saying, "Jenna, if your team gets out in less time, I will get the coffee in the morning for a month. If my team does it, you get the morning coffee for a month."

Jenna quickly said, "Done deal."

Then Jack said, "I know where you're coming from, Jenna, but I have to regretfully inform you that Sophia can read *hanzi* as fast as I can. She may not be able to speak and understand Chinese that well but *hanzi* she can. However, I think we have a real competition; this should be fun."

Just then Marcus's cell phone beeped and looking at the text message, he said, "It's from Yohana. There's a regatta on Saturday and she wants me to crew."

With a smile on her face, Jenna quickly said, "That's fine with me, as long as you get my coffee before you leave in the morning." Then all laughed together.

⟨Φ⟩

Both teams exited the escape rooms within minutes of each other. But Jenna's team was the first out. As Marcus's team came out, Jenna quickly called out, "With cream and sugar, remember." And all laughed again.

Cell phones were not permitted in the escape rooms and as they all exited, they went to the basket they had put them in before entering. Marcus's was beeping as he took it out of the basket and looking down, he saw it was from José Rodriguez. Reading it, his face went white and he called Jenna over to read. **Nunzio and two associates were convicted of kidnapping and attempted murder. Adriana escaped capture and was not prosecuted.** Looking at Jenna, Marcus said, "We made it through the escape rooms but it appears we have not yet escaped from the Gambioni vendetta."

⟨Φ⟩

It was Friday night happy hour at the yacht club. The Petersons and Wongs were sharing a table with LiJing. Much discussion was going on about the escape room experiences they had had. LiJing complimented them all by telling them that she felt both teams did extremely well. She indicated that it was the first time they had tried this escape room test and with it working so well, they definitely would be utilizing the escape room concept of the two future tests.

A pitcher of margaritas sat on the table and LiJing stood, picking up the pitcher and topping off everyone's glass, saying, "I propose a toast to the next phase of your training, Malay. May it go as well as Mandarin."

They all stood, saying, "Here, here."

Sitting down, they were surprised to see Yohana come running across the room and pull up a chair next to Marcus, saying, "Marcus, I'm so glad I caught you, I forgot to tell you tomorrow's regatta is a race to Santa Cruz and back. We'll be spending the night in Santa Cruz and returning on Sunday. It can be a six- or seven-hour sail in either direction depending on winds and how the course will be laid out. The Santa Cruz Yacht Club will be hosting us for dinner and we will spend the night onboard. Juan has booked us a mooring at a marina close to the yacht club. As you are well aware, there's plenty of sleeping room on the New-porter and if we have good wind and can maybe make a spinnaker run we should be back by early afternoon Sunday." Then looking at Jenna with a mischievous smile she said, "Don't worry, Jenna, I'll take good care of him and bring him back safe."

All eyes at the table were first on Yohana and then on Jenna. The reaction was as expected. Her face reflected deep worry and with a somewhat mocking voice, she said, "I'm sure you will. It sounds like quite an escape."

Yohana quickly got up and looking at Marcus, said, "See you in the morning. We set sail at 9:00 so try to get there early. Adios."

LiJing, sensing what could be a difficult situation, decided to quickly refocus consideration of Marcus's escape, saying, "Marcus, the smuggling event that you are anticipating must be coming soon. I would be very aware of Yohana's and Juan's activities while in Santa Cruz. I wouldn't be surprised if part of this trip was to make final arrangements for delivery of their future cargo. Due to the closeness of Silicon Valley, Santa Cruz would be a logical drop-off point. I'm sure the whole time you are there you will either be with Yohana or Juan or both. I would suggest as soon as you know what marina you're going to be docked in, contact José Rodriguez. Either he or he could have somebody else be up there to possibly follow around either José or Yohana if they split off from you. Just a thought but it could pay off."

"Good thought," responded Marcus, "I'll definitely do that. Tomorrow night could be very interesting."

CHAPTER 11

SANTA CRUZ

T he alarm went off at six and Marcus crawled out of bed, slipped on some sweats and went down to the hotel breakfast room for coffee and danish. As he got back in the room, he was greeted by Jenna as she rolled over in bed, "Marcus, what time is it?"

"It's about 6:15. Brought you coffee and a danish. You can share with me while I dress. I'll have to be on my way shortly. Yohana said I should be down by the boat by seven. Race starts promptly at nine and we have to motor out and get in position with sails up."

"This could be a long day for you, Marcus, and hopefully, a lot of fun."

"Yes, it will be at least a seven-hour run up to Santa Cruz and if the wind is the way it normally is, we probably will be sailing into it. That will put us on a close reach, tacking all the way."

"Where will you spend the night?"

"I'm sure onboard. There is plenty of room on *Spirit* and the Santa Cruz Yacht Club is hosting us for dinner. So once we get there, it will be dinner at the yacht club and then back to the boat and into the sack, as the sail back will be just as long. Hopefully we will be going with the wind most of the way back so we might be able to make a little better time. Jenna, don't get dressed. I can walk to the boat from here but plan on picking me up tomorrow. I'll call you on the cell phone when we get close to Monterey." Marcus gave Jenna a quick kiss and after they finished their coffee, picked up the small bag he had packed the night before saying, "Bye for now, love you much," as he opened the door leaving the suite.

Jenna then called out, "Safe trip, have fun."

It was only about a 20-minute walk and as Marcus approached *Spirit* he saw Juan installing the sails and running the lines. Yohana was sitting in the cockpit reading through the regatta brochure. As he approached the boat, Yohana called out, "Welcome aboard. Stow your gear and get comfortable. It's going to be a hot one today and the sun will be on our back most of the way. T-shirts and swim suits are the order of the day."

As she stood up to give Marcus a hand, he was surprised to see she obviously had nothing more than a bikini and a white t-shirt on. Instead of her usual ponytail, she had hair clips allowing her hair to flow down. Her shapely body made her appear as attractive as he'd ever seen her. *Careful now,* he thought.

Hopping onboard he immediately went below, dropping his bag and taking off his slacks. He was happy he had worn a t-shirt and his bathing suit underneath. As he came back up on deck, Juan was releasing the bow line and Yohana had already started the engine. She immediately called out, "Get the stern line, Marcus, and we will be on our way. You will be in the cockpit with me and work the main and the mizzen. Juan will be forward working the jib."

As they motored out, they were heading directly into the wind, allowing for easy raising of the sails by Marcus and Juan. Shortly they were underway moving into position for the start. Yohana shut down the engine and put *Spirit* on a course to cross the starting line when the starting gun went off, but not before.

Initially the wind was blowing straight from Santa Cruz, requiring a close reach and lots of tacking to maintain course. Yohana stood at the wheel while Marcus was in and out of the cockpit working the mizzen and the main on each tack. He paid little attention to the occasional touching he received from Yohana as he passed by.

As the sun rose generating considerable heat on their backs, and their exertion required for sail handling, they were soon wet with perspiration. Eventually the wind began to shift coming further east of Santa Cruz, allowing for a broad reach to their mark and Yohana called out, "Marcus, I think we can maintain this starboard tack for a while. Take the helm."

Switching positions, Yohana went to the high side of the cockpit and grabbed a water. Drinking part of it, she poured the rest on her head and body to cool off, the wet t-shirt clearly revealing she was wearing no bra. She called out to Marcus to get his attention, saying, "Don't mind me Marcus, I'm just going to do some stretches to loosen up." And she went into some very provocative movements. *Oh boy,* thought Marcus, *this is a "come on" if I ever saw one. This could get very tempting. I've got to concentrate on sailing.*

For the remainder of the trip Marcus and Yohana took turns at the helm and Juan resupplied all with food and beverage from the galley when the angle of the boat permitted. The overall sail to Santa Cruz put a huge demand on the physical capabilities of *Spirit's* crew. After crossing the finish line, they dropped the sails as they approached Santa Cruz harbor. Yohana turned on the engine as they passed the Walton Lighthouse on the entrance jetty.

The V-dock marina was just inside the entrance and Marcus and Juan worked to stow the sails as Yohana motored *Spirit* into their designated mooring. One of the marina workers helped them with tie up and directed them to where the bathhouse was, indicating that hot showers were available and gave her three plastic key cards, saying, "Here, these will open the gate to the docks and the bathhouse door. The marina is quite secure."

"How far is the yacht club?" asked Yohana, "And what's the best way to get there?"

"It's a bit of a walk down this side of the harbor but you can take a water taxi that you can pick up at the end of the pier. It continues to run until eight at night. The yacht club is actually on the upper street and overlooks the harbor but there's a tram going up to it from the yacht club dock area."

Juan came back to the cockpit, saying, "Yohana, you and Marcus go on up and shower and go on to the yacht club. I'll be along a little later. I want to top off the fresh water tank and check the engine so we're ready to go in the morning."

"Good plan," said Yohana. And with that, she and Marcus grabbed their bags and went on up to the bathhouse. The single bathhouse entry door opened to a small sitting area and two archways, one going to the men's locker room and the other to the ladies. Yohana said, "Looks like we have the place to ourselves. I don't think there's anyone else here."

"Let's meet back here when you're ready," said Marcus. And with that, they both peeled off and went into their respective locker rooms. Marcus had opened a locker, put his cloths in and shed his wet t-shirt and swimsuit. Grabbing two fresh towels from the towel rack, he started toward the showers when he was startled by a bloodcurdling scream from Yohana.

"Yohana, what's the matter?" he called as he raced into the ladies shower area.

He was immediately embraced by the voluptuous wet body of Yohana who gave him a very passionate kiss and said, "Your prize for doing an outstanding sailing job today." Though his groin immediately responded, his mind went into overdrive thinking, *I can't do this. I have got to break away.*

⌀

Hand in hand, Marcus and Yohana went down the harbor walkway towards the Santa Cruz Yacht Club. They walked in silence but Marcus's brain was spinning.

I can't believe what happened, he thought, and the bathhouse activity kept spinning in review in his mind.

It was a longer walk to the yacht club tram than Marcus and Yohana anticipated. In fact, they arrived at the tram the same time Juan did, he arriving by water taxi of course. "What took you so long?" Juan said as he approached from where he got off the water taxi. "I squared away the boat, got showered, got dressed and got down here the same time as you."

"It's a little bit of a longer walk than we anticipated. I'm sure you saw that when you came down by water taxi," said Yohana.

"And there's no question. We take the water taxi home." chimed in Marcus.

The tram came to a halt at a wide deck on the side and front of the yacht club that overlooked the harbor area and Yohana immediately went to the table adjacent to the entry that held a multitude of name tags. "They are alphabetical by boat name," someone said and Yohana immediately found theirs. Handing them to Marcus and Juan, she said, "Looks like we are officially here as guests so I believe we can go in and eat."

There was a huge queue at the buffet table and every table inside and out was partially or fully full. "We may not be sitting together," said Marcus as he gazed around the room.

"Not a problem," said Juan. "We get to meet people. It's sort of fun."

"Well, if I see and have to sit with that bastard that was sailing the Star boat that forced us to come about ahead of the last mark, I'll probably do something drastic to him that I will regret."

"Calm yourself, Yohana," said Marcus, then, "Oh, hold my place in line. I think I see somebody I know." Looking across the room, he had spotted senior CIA Agent Brady Nelson, who he had worked with on his last assignment. *I have no idea why he's up here but I have got to get to him before he recognizes me and comes over,* he thought. *I have got to let him know that I'm undercover. He could blow the whole thing if he mentioned our CIA relationship.* "Brady, it's great to see you," said Marcus as he came up to the table that Brady was sitting at. "What brings you to Santa Cruz?"

"Hi Marcus, I might ask you the same. I finished up a case in San Francisco and came down here just for fun before going back to New York. My membership in the Seawanhaka Yacht Club on Long Island got me in. What about you? I thought you and Jenna were going to school at the Presidio."

"We are. We joined the Monterey Peninsula Yacht Club for fun and it's currently conducting a regatta, Monterey to Santa Cruz and return. Most of the people you see here are members of the Monterey Peninsula Yacht Club and we sail back tomorrow morning. I love sailing and have raced before and I'm currently crewing on a Newporter ketch that's in the race. I'm in the food line with the skipper and her brother. I didn't know you sailed. Look, if seats open up at your table, I'll bring them over." Then bending down, Marcus whispered in Brady's ear. "They are associated with the local Mexican Mafia and have no idea that I'm CIA. In addition to going to school, I recently got another assignment that involves them. I'll fill you in on it later."

With that said, Marcus quickly returned to his place in the buffet line saying to Yohana and Juan, "He's a close friend of mine from New York; also a sailor. He's here on vacation and as a member of a yacht club on Long Island got in here to eat. The people at his table were finishing up and he said he would save us seats when they left. I'll introduce you. He's a nice guy."

⟨D⟩

The conversation at the table was pretty much about sailing and the Mendezes explaining what they did in Monterey. Brady being an avid golfer was excited when he heard Juan was a caddie at Pebble Beach and the conversation quickly changed to questions about who Juan had caddied for. Finishing their meal, Yohana announced, "We'll leave you two to chat as I'm going up to the judges table to file a complaint about that Star boat that caused us to miss the last mark. I need Juan along as a witness. We will pick up some more dessert dishes on the way back to the table." As soon as they were gone, Marcus brought Brady up to speed on his new assignment and why he was undercover with Yohana and Juan.

"Well, Marcus," said Brady, "If you have to get close to a Mafia adversary, a looker like Yohana is not too bad to get close to. I bet Jenna is not too pleased."

"She isn't. I keep telling her it's all in the line of duty, nothing more than that, but you know her, she's as jealous as they come. Look, maybe you can help me out. I have a gut feel that Juan is going to leave early and make a contact while we're up here. If the opportunity presents itself, maybe you could follow him. Maybe offer to take him where he wants to go since you have a rental car."

"Okay, we can give it a try. Oops, here they come."

As Yohana and Juan approached the table, they each were carrying two portions of strawberry cake. Juan finished his before anyone else and as predicted, looking at Marcus and Yohana, said, "Look, I have an errand to run. I'll see you back at the boat." Looking at Brady, he said, "Great meeting you. If you ever get back this way, maybe we can play a round at Pebble Beach."

"That would be great," said Brady, "Look, I'm about to leave myself. Can I give you a lift? I've got a rental car out front."

"Thanks, that would be great," said Juan and then looking at Marcus with a sly grin, he said, "I won't be too late and I'll call out before I board the boat."

"Marcus, say hi to Jenna for me. Hope to see you soon," said Brady. As soon as they left, Marcus pulled out his cell phone, saying to Yohana, "I've got to call Jenna. I'm going out on the deck. I think that's better reception."

"I'll go get us some coffee. I'll see you out there," said Yohana.

Marcus found an empty table on the deck and called Jenna. He filled her in on all the events on the sail up, dinner at the yacht club, and Brady Nelson showing up. He was careful not to mention the activities in the shower. He was just finishing up the call when Yohana returned with two coffees and, setting them down on the table, called out loudly, "I'm taking good care of him, Jenna."

Hoping Jenna hadn't heard that, Marcus ended the call with, "Bye for now. I'll call you in the morning before we leave. Love you."

⊕

Getting into his rental car, Brady said, "Where to, Juan?"

"It's the Avocado store. I'm having a problem with my phone. I looked it up before we came. It's up on Petrero Street."

"Give me the address. I'll plug it in the GPS," said Brady. It turned out it was only a few blocks away. As they pulled up in front of the shop, Brady said, "Look, Juan, I have the time. If you like, I can wait for you and take you back to the yacht club or wherever you have the *Spirit* docked."

"That would be great," said Juan, "I'll only be a short while."

"Not a problem. I may go in and browse. I'm always interested to see what new products they have." Inside the shop Brady started looking at the watches and new phones at the front of the store while keeping an eye on Juan. Juan went directly to the technicians at the back of the shop and was immediately escorted through a door to a back area. Brady immediately texted Marcus, **I'm not sure this is what you want, but we are at an Avocado store and he was taken into a back area. He said he needed his phone fixed.**

Thanks. We will talk tomorrow. I will call you. Marcus texted back.

ⅅ

"Yohana, we better hurry if we're going to catch that last water taxi back," said Marcus as he got up from the table.

"You're right. Let's go," said Yohana. "Was that text you just got important? You had a serious expression on your face when you read it."

"No, no problem. Jenna just saying goodnight."

The trip back to the Marina was quick and with *Spirit* plugged into dock power, Juan had left the lights on in the pilothouse and the main cabin. In addition the marina had dock lighting on all the slips so finding their yacht and getting onboard turned out to be easy in the dark. "Juan usually sleeps in the pilothouse," said Yohana as they got on board. "You can have any of the bunks in the main cabin. I'll be sleeping in the forward cabin," and then with a mischievous grin, she followed with, "and you're welcome anytime." As she went forward she thought, *and if you don't, when your asleep I'll come up and look at your phone to see just what Jenna said to you to make you not want me.*

Chapter 12

The Trip Home

M arcus awoke with a start. There was the smell of bacon frying, the rocking of the boat, and the pop of a Pillsbury biscuit dough container all at once that brought him to consciousness.

Peeking out of his sleeping bag he saw the back of Juan busy cooking in the small galley on the Newporter. He quickly called out, "Juan, what time is it? I must've overslept. I'm sorry. Where is Yohana?"

Turning around with a somewhat disturbed look on his face, Juan responded, "It's 6:30. Yohana is up at the showers and the race home starts at eight. I would've woken you earlier but Yohana insisted on letting you sleep. Now you won't have time to shower, as we have got to eat, take off the sail covers and motor out to the start. Luckily the wind is from the Northeast so the first leg will be on a broad reach and I suspect the next leg will be running with the wind. Possibly a long spinnaker run. This should make for easy sail handling initially. Yohana has already eaten so when she gets back, we move out. Now get your ass in gear. I'll have breakfast ready in a few minutes."

Trying for a little levity as he crawled out of his sleeping bag, Marcus responded, "Aye, Aye, sir."

◍

As Yohana showered, her mind was spinning. *I don't understand what I read on Marcus's cell phone last night. That text was obviously not from Jenna. it didn't make sense to me but it mentioned the Avocado store where Juan was supposed to meet with whoever we are going to be turning our cargo over to. But I couldn't even tell who it was from. Do I question Marcus about it? Do I tell Juan? I'll have to think about this some more. I better get moving. We have a race to win.*

◍

Juan and Marcus had finished breakfast and Juan had gone forward to the sail storage compartment in the bow. Marcus had just finished rinsing the dishes and was about to go up on deck when his cell phone rang. It was a text from Jenna saying, **Good morning**. He quickly typed a response, saying, **Contact Brady, get info, pass on, later.** Then clicking his phone off and stowing it in his bag, he quickly went up on deck.

Juan called out, "I'll raise the jib now and we can raise the main and mizzen when we clear the lighthouse at the end of the entrance jetty."

"Okay, I see Yohana coming down the wharf. I will start the engine and get the stern line if you get the bow line as soon as she gets onboard and we can be off," responded Marcus. As Yohana boarded, Marcus said, "Go down below and get changed. I'll take her out."

"Are you okay with that," said Yohana.

"Look, the time we spent coming up here, and the time I spent at the helm, I think I pretty much know this boat. By the way, when you come back up, I have a thin windbreaker in my bag. If you bring it up, I would appreciate it, thanks much."

Yohana went below, changing into a bikini and t-shirt and was about to come up when she remembered Marcus's request. She opened his bag, rummaged around to find the windbreaker and saw his cell phone. Curiosity got the better of her and she popped it open to look at the messages. Seeing the exchange with Jenna, she thought, *What's going on? I've got to question him about this. I'm not sure how I go about it but I think I'll hold off and question him when we get back. For now I want to keep him focused on sailing and me.*

◍

Jenna was delighted to get Marcus's text and talk to Brady. As she saw it, the undercover assignment could be over and Marcus's cuddling up to Yohana could stop. After all the Avocado Corporation is obviously the company that's paying for the smuggling of Chinese into the US and that's what the agency wanted us to determine.

She immediately set up a conference call with Station Chief Alonzo and local FBI contact Rodriguez. The time difference between New York and Monterey gave her a little problem but by mid-morning she was able to accomplish it. After reporting to them both what Brady had discovered, Station Chief Alonzo said, "That's great intelligence, but it's got to be validated. We've got to witness the actual smuggling of Chinese technical personnel as well as Avocado personnel receiving them and possibly paying for the service. Tell Marcus to continue undercover." This was followed by an immediate click terminating the conference call. Jenna was not at all happy with the response.

⟨⟨D⟩⟩

Yohana came into the cockpit and took the helm as they rounded the Walton Lighthouse at the end of the Santa Cruz harbor jetty. Juan raised the mizzen, Marcus raised the main and Yohana cut the engine. This put *Spirit* under sail in a broad reach headed east of the starting mark. Yohana's plan was to come about into a broad reach south-west and cross the starting mark as the gun fired at exactly 8 o'clock.

There was silence in the cockpit. Both Marcus and Juan were at their posts with the mizzen and mainsail. Yohana was carefully watching the other boats and *Spirit's* position relative to the start. Suddenly the silence was broken when Yohana yelled, "Coming about," and spun the tiller wheel to take *Spirit* in the opposite direction. *Spirit* quickly swung into an easterly direction and crossed the start at about 10 seconds after the gun.

Marcus and Juan screamed together, "Outstanding."

Marcus followed with, "You're truly a racing skipper, Yohana."

With a big smile on her face and not letting go of the wheel, she bowed to each of them, saying, "Thank you, thank you, thank you."

"Looks like we're going to be on this reach for a while and with the sun coming up, I think it's going to be a hot one. Yohana, I'm going to go below and get rid of this windbreaker and slacks," said Marcus and he quickly went below. He found his bag open and his cell phone up on the table. Then he thought, *She must've taken my phone out when she was looking for my windbreaker. I wonder if she looked at my texts. That could be a problem. She's been all business on deck this morning and not a hint of what happened in the showers. I hope my cover hasn't been blown. Maybe I can overcome that if I pay her a little attention, indicating I might be interested in getting closer.*

Back in the cockpit, he sat down close to her saying, "It was a spectacular bit of sailing you just did at the start, and may I tell you, you looked quite nice last night at the yacht club. I really enjoyed being there with you."

Yohana quickly turned, giving Marcus a quick kiss and said, "Thank you, I enjoyed being there with you." Then her mind began to spin, thinking, *I believe I may be getting to him. Sorry, Jenna, I think I can woo him away. I'm not sure about those messages on his cell phone but I'm not going to worry about them for now. I'm much more interested in getting it on with Marcus.*

"Marcus, have you ever sailed at night," she said. "It's a bit of a challenge but in certain weather it can be quite nice. Especially if there's a full moon."

"That could be a little dicey," said Marcus. "How do you see the sails?"

"Well, in addition to the boat's running lights, I have two mini floods positioned to shine up on the main and mizzen, in addition to helping you sail, it's a better indication to other boats that you're here. That's especially true if you're out in the ocean close to the shipping lanes."

"Boy, you sure have *Spirit* equipped to do just about anything. I'm impressed," said Marcus.

"Juan, could you go down and check the GPS. After we round the next mark, it should be a straight shot to Monterey. Get me the heading. If the wind holds the current direction, it could be a spinnaker run the whole time. That way we might make Monterey early afternoon. Marcus, you could go forward and get the spinnaker ready. As soon as Juan checks our position and gives me the heading, he will come forward to help you. With the way the wind is blowing, I'll come over and will fly with the spinnaker pole to starboard and mizzen and mainsail to port. We could really get some speed," called out Yohana.

After getting *Spirit* on course, Marcus and Juan were midship making further adjustments on the spinnaker pole and spinnaker sheet for max performance. As it filled, the forward thrust caused the bow to start to go down and Yohana called out, "Secure all the sheets and get back here as quickly as possible." All three settled back in the cockpit. Yohana was still at the helm and *Spirit* came to a level position and picked up speed. "If this wind holds force and direction, we could hit a hull speed of 11 knots. Monterey here we come, maybe as early as 3 PM," said Yohana.

⏭

The wind held direction and with minor course changes, they were able to fly the spinnaker the entire run to Monterey. Crossing the finish, Yohana changed course, and Juan and Marcus went forward to raise the jib, blanketing the spinnaker and slacking the afterguy line so the spinnaker pole went forward, dumping the remaining air from the spinnaker. Marcus slowly lowered it while Juan stuffed it into its bag.

Yohana changed course again and they were able to lower the remaining sails to motor into the Monterey Marina. Marcus got his cell phone and called Jenna only to find out they had been watching the race and she and the Wongs were already down on the wharf waiting for them. Jack Wong helped them tie up and Marcus went below and got his gear.

Back in the cockpit Yohana said, "Marcus, you did great. It was awesome having you crew." And then she gave him quick kiss on the cheek. Seeing Jenna on the wharf she called out, "See, I brought him back safely." Then looking at Marcus, she said, "Juan and I will secure *Spirit*. You go on over to the yacht club. As soon as we're finished, we will join you. I'm curious to see how we did but it will be a while before all the boats are in and the judges finish the scoring."

⏭

As they stowed the sails and cleaned and locked up *Spirit*, Yohana told Juan what she spotted on Marcus's phone and her concern for what it might mean. "You know, I sort of like Marcus. He is an excellent sailor and I enjoy flirting with him but other than sailing and the yacht club, we have no idea what his and Jenna's background is, as well as the Wongs. We know they go to the language school here and they are from back east but that's all. What if they are associated with the law in some way. We could be in deep dung. I sure as hell don't want to end up where our father is by doing the activities that he calls on us to do. This is getting a little dangerous. Drug smuggling we help him with and I always felt we could say we had no idea what was going on. It's probably a little naïve. We're never here when the drugs get unloaded, so I thought we were okay. Also, I am a little scared of some of the men he sends over to unload the drugs. I get the feeling that they have no qualms about utilizing murder to get their way or to take care of anybody who appears to be inhibiting their activity. Oh, I just don't know. What're your thoughts?"

"Well, Yohana, you know that Marcus as well as most members of the yacht club knows that our father was arrested years back as he was head of the local La eMe. So even though most members know we were raised in a Mexican Mafia family, I don't think any suspect that we are active in it now."

"And we certainly don't want that to change," said Yohana. "We better get over to the yacht club."

⊕

As expected, the yacht club was crowded but in a corner of the room the Petersons and Wongs spotted LiJing alone at a table waving and they immediately went over. "Welcome back," she said. "I knew it would be crowded so I got here early to reserve a table. A pitcher of margaritas should be here shortly and Marcus, please tell us all about it."

The margaritas arrived and Marcus began to relate the saga. He covered the whole trip giving the details of the race up, being cut off by another competing boat before rounding the last mark, the activities at the yacht club and the sail home today. Of course, he was careful not to mention the shower activities with Yohana.

"How exciting," said Jack. "What will happen about being cut off?"

"Yohana filed a complaint and when she talked to the judges at the yacht club, they said they were aware and were securing information on just what happened. One of them on the judge's boat witnessed the whole maneuver of us having to go back around the last mark. I don't know what that will mean or how the scoring goes, but I'm sure we will find out tonight."

Through all the discussion that when on, Jenna was careful not to mention her discussion with Station Chief Alonzo. Juan and Yohana arrived at the table carrying two glasses and another pitcher of margaritas. The rest of the table raised their glasses and yelled together, "Congratulations. We heard you ran a dynamite race."

"Thank you, thank you," said Yohana, "and let me say Marcus did a wonderful job. He is truly a great sailor. Incidentally, I stopped at the judges table on the way in and luckily one of the judges on the judging boat clocked the time it took us to go back around the last mark and subtracted it from our total time. Judges thought rather than make a big issue about it they would just do that and no one would be the wiser. That avoids getting into the issue of whether we were cut off on purpose or by mistake and it avoids a possible embarrassment by the other yacht club member. So, overall we should have done quite well in our class as well as overall."

⑪

Finally home in their apartment, they settled down in their bed and entered into evening conversation before going to sleep.

"Marcus, it's really great that you guys took first place in your class and I was surprised how well you did overall. Those smaller racing sailboats are fast. You did pretty well."

"You're right, but even though *Spirit* is really a cruising boat, Yohana has made a lot of modifications on the boat to make her quite efficient when sailing in a race. And Yohana herself is one good experienced sailor. There's no question about it."

"Oh, I didn't tell you but when I got back to Station Chief Alonzo and Rodriguez, he says the FBI and the CIA are concerned you don't have enough information. The fact that it appears Avocado Corporation's funding the operation still needs validation that they are and that Chinese are being smuggled in. It can't be that it just appears to be. Basically, you are supposed to get back undercover, continue to try to befriend Yohana, and gain her trust so she involves you in the operation. Needless to say, I'm not excited about that."

"That may be a problem," said Marcus and he then related to Jenna his suspicion that Yohana had seen the texts on his cell phone. Then rolling over and taking Jenna in his arms he said, "That's tomorrow's problem. It's time for sleep."

CHAPTER 13

STRANGE INPUT
FROM AFAR

LiJing was surprised to receive a classified communiqué from her father in Singapore at the Presidio. It had been some years since her father retired from the US Consulate in Singapore and since that time all communication with her family had been on her private email, phone, and occasional written letters from her mother.

She was apprised of the communication from the admin office at the Presidio at about 5 PM, which would've been about 9 AM in Singapore. The message simply requested a call be made to a specific phone number at the Consulate on a secure government line the following day at precisely 5 PM Pacific standard time.

LiJing thought this was unusual, immediately thinking there might be some sort of a family emergency. Then calming her immediate emotions and seeing that it came from the US Consulate in Singapore, she realized it most likely would have nothing to do with the family. In the past any time either one of them had a health issue or anything else, they would immediately call her on her personal line so this must be something entirely different. She went home somewhat perplexed but in control, resisting her desire to pick up her cell phone and place a personal call.

At home she spent most of the evening on the Internet searching all sorts of news media about what was going on in Singapore, if anything. *I wonder if I should call Marcus and Jenna. They, being CIA, may know something that isn't common knowledge about Singapore. No, I better wait till tomorrow and see them in class. If they did know something, they wouldn't say it over the phone, I'm sure.*

⚙

The following day in class LiJing did have time to chat with Marcus and Jenna during lunch hour and told them of the communication she received from her father and asked if they were aware of anything going on in Singapore to which they said no, but they would certainly check if she received any more information from her dad.

No further conversation occurred during the day and at five sharp LiJing went to her office and called on a Presidio secure line to Singapore. The routing of the call took several minutes but eventually she heard her father's voice greeting her. "Father, is everything alright? What seems to be the matter? I was really concerned when I got your message," said LiJing.

"Not to worry, LiJing. It is just some information I came across that I felt you should know based on what you told me about your young CIA students. We have to be concerned about what we say publicly in Singapore so I thought it best to talk with you from the US consulate. Even though I'm retired, I have access there."

"What is this all about?" asked LiJing, totally surprised.

"You remember our good friend Jack Yang, the travel agent?"

"Yes."

"Well, we were chatting the other day and he was telling me about how he is handling many young Chinese engineers coming in from mainland China and booking travel to Acapulco, Mexico. He indicated that all this started several months ago when your country stopped allowing immigration from China, especially students and technical personnel. These were typical personnel that had in the past been applying for American visas here in Singapore. They would come here from

Beijing and apply for American visas at the US consulate. It obviously was easier than trying to get a visa in China proper. Arranging for tourist visas to Mexico from here was quite easy for him. When he mentioned that he never booked return flights, it began to pique my curiosity. Remember, foreign intrigue has always been my hobby. Well, I immediately passed it on here at the Consulate but I'm not sure what they will do with the information. Again, remembering your students, I thought it might be worthwhile passing this on to you."

"Well, Father, that is intriging, and I will pass it on to my students. I can't discuss the details now but they are involved with a situation that's currently going on right here in Monterey. Is there a way I can initiate a call to you at the consulate should they want more information?"

"Not a problem, just send me a regular email saying when you will be calling me and follow the same process we did today."

⦶

Marcus and Jenna had just gotten into their apartment when Jenna's phone rang and to her surprise it was LiJing, who briefly related what she had heard from her dad.

"LiJing, we have to pass this along to Station Chief Alonzo and Rodriguez. I'll see if I can set up a conference call tomorrow at our lunch break. You can relate to them what you told us. Knowing the routing of the cargo could be critical to their overall investigation and hearing it from you is vital, as they probably would want you to get follow-up information from your dad," said Jenna.

"Not a problem," said LiJing. "I will break the class at 12:30 for lunch and we can go to my office and make the call."

⦶

The Sardine Factory opens for dinner at three and it was five to as Yohana rushed from the parking structure at Cannery Row to get to work. She wasn't looking forward to another chewing out like the one she got the last time she was late. Halfway up the stairs to the front door, her cell phone rang. *Should I answer?* she thought and, taking it from her pocketbook, she saw it was from her dad.

"Hello, Father, I can't speak now. I'm about to be late for work. I . . ."

She was immediately interrupted by her father saying, "Yohana, a human shipment is ready. I need to know the next scheduled regatta that will allow you to make a pickup. I will call tomorrow." And then the phone went dead. *Why doesn't he let me talk to him,* she thought. *He just gives cryptic orders and hangs up. I just don't understand. Now however it's probably just as well, as I don't want to be late for work.*

⨁

LiJing's office was small but Marcus and Jenna pulled up two chairs in front of her desk and she sat behind. There were two phone units on her desk, one black and one red. She slid the red one over in front of Jenna, saying, "This is a secure line. You should be able to connect to the secure line at the CIA office in New York."

Jenna made the call and Station Chief Alonzo immediately answered. "Sir, I have LiJing Chen here who has received some interesting information from her father in Singapore, which I believe could be important to our case. I will let her explain."

LiJing then recited the discussion she had had with her father which led to an immediate question and answer conversation among all present. This finished with Station Chief Alonzo saying, "This may or may not be possible, but please tell your father that if he could get the following information on the most recent group of Chinese that his friend provided travel arrangements for, it would be extremely beneficial to our investigation. That is, their names, their profession or if a student, their field of study, and whether they are military and/or CCP. The last two would probably be very difficult to find out but extremely beneficial to us if he could."

The call ended and Marcus looked at LiJing, saying, "It appears the ball is in your court and if you get answers, you certainly can go directly to Station Chief Alonzo. Keep us informed, however, as it could affect how we deal with Yohana's next cargo."

CHAPTER 14

AN UNFOLDING
RELATIONSHIP

A weekend routine began to develop with the Wongs and Petersons. On Saturday, Marcus would sail with Yohana in the local regatta or just on their own. A crew of three was definitely required on *Spirit* when in competition. Marcus was becoming more and more experienced with the boat and its capabilities. Sometimes Jack Wong would go along if Juan had to caddie at Pebble Beach. Jenna and Sophia would go shopping in Monterey or Carmel. At times, Jack would accompany them if they drove into the city.

The primary goal was for Marcus to gain the trust of Yohana. In that light, a definite relationship began to develop between Marcus and Yohana. In addition to discussions about sailing, often their conversations included Yohana and Juan describing their growing up in Monterey. Marcus was careful to keep the conversation focused on them and not him. Emotionally their feelings began to go in different directions. Marcus began to feel like they were family, even occasionally calling her by his sister's name. However, Yohana continued to be physically attracted to Marcus, making romantic advances whenever the opportunity presented itself. Declining these advances, without jeopardizing the close relationship he was trying to establish, became more of a challenge every day that they were together.

Contrary to the Italian Mafia, where family was most always shielded from the crime family's activities, it appeared that in Mexican Mafia families most everyone was aware to some extent of the crime family's activities.

It was Saturday morning and the Wongs and Petersons were sharing an early breakfast. "Marcus, what time are you going sailing today?" asked Jenna.

"Yohana told me I didn't need to be down there until about 11 o'clock. Juan had an early tee time at Pebble Beach and wouldn't be able to get to the marina until then. It will be a more demanding sail today as she plans to go out of the bay into the ocean. She said she'd like me to experience sailing in the ocean as the winds and seas are entirely different than the bay. Further, we will be sailing back between four and five in the afternoon, as that is about the peak tide change. Evidently at this time of the year, the tide change can be fairly severe and sailing against the current can be a little tricky, especially when the afternoon wind comes up."

"Sounds like you're going to have an exciting day," said Jack. "I wish I could be along, but I promised the girls I would drive them into the city today. You will have to give us a full report at cocktail hour tonight."

"Yes, it could be somewhat riveting. Sailing on Long Island Sound back east, I've never had to deal with tide currents," said Marcus.

"By the way, how's the Yohana relationship coming?" asked Sophia. At that question you could see Jenna's face go sour, but she didn't say a word.

"It's somewhat fascinating, in that she, well, both she and Juan, have been telling me how it was growing up in Monterey. It seems that even though they were teenagers at the time their father was arrested, they were aware of his criminal activity. They weren't really sure what it was, but they became aware when he bought *Spirit*. They were only allowed to sail it on weekends, as during the week it could be gone for one or two days. He never told them exactly what he was doing but did say it was illegal and it was best that they didn't know. When he was arrested, the authorities never bothered with them," responded Marcus.

"Any mention of what they're doing now?" asked Jack.

"Not yet," responded Marcus. "Hopefully, she'll begin to trust me and maybe divulge family secrets. That's what I am trying for. There is always a flirtatious manner about her but I'm beginning to treat her more like a sister."

"I bet," said Jack with a mischievous grin.

"Let's not go there." chimed in Jenna and the breakfast conversation stopped for a pause.

⊕

Marcus got down to the yacht club marina a little before 11. He saw no sign of Juan but Yohana was on deck speaking to someone he'd never seen before. The conversation was in Spanish so he couldn't understand what was going on but it appeared to be heated and Yohana didn't appear to be happy. Marcus immediately jumped aboard saying aloud, "Is there a problem, Yohana?"

Startled, Yohana turned to Marcus and said, "it's okay, not a problem."

The stranger, however, turned to him saying something in Spanish in a very angry tone. Marcus, considerably larger in size than the stranger, approached him saying, "I think you better leave."

Yohana immediately said something in Spanish to the stranger, Marcus suspecting she was translating what he had said. The stranger jumped off the boat onto the dock and again said something in Spanish to Yohana and walked off. Marcus immediately asked Yohana, "What was that all about? Can I help?"

"I'm sorry you witnessed that," said Yohana and her mind went into high gear. *What do I do now?* she thought. *That was Raul, one of my father's gang members. He can be ruthless; he would have no concern in wasting someone. Do I lie and make up a story or do I tell him about my father and what we do for him. I'm really not sure about him to try a story.* "Not to worry, Marcus; he is just family, and can really be obnoxious at times. They are always trying to borrow my boat but I won't let them. They keep asking and they sometimes get difficult when I refuse.

However, for what just happened now, watch yourself from here on; he can be a very nasty individual."

Before any other conversation could occur, Juan showed up and all three immediately went to work getting *Spirit* ready to sail. As Marcus worked the sails with Juan, his mind began to reflect on what just happened. *I can't be sure because it was so dark but that so-called family member I think was the one Jenna decked the other night when we saw them unloading Spirit. And if it was, I'm sure he'll be gunning for me.*

⊕

The sail out of the bay was quite normal but once they hit the open water, things changed rapidly. The sea quickly changed to what would be called a sea state three. Wave action would be 2 to 3 1/2 feet with occasional whitecaps and the wind was about 7 to 10 knots.

Marcus had never sailed in this type of condition before and began to see it was quite different. They went out about 2 1/2 miles, making a grand circle. Yohana had Marcus at the helm while she handled the mizzen and Juan the main. This allowed Marcus to see how *Spirit* handled in various wind conditions and direction of the sea state. Completing the circle, they headed back into the bay. About this time the tide was going out so in addition to facing wind and wave action they were bucking a current. Maintaining a bearing became an issue. You would be sailing in one direction but the angle of the tide would be forcing you in another. You had to compensate in your bearing, which became a bit of a challenge. Yohana was constantly giving orders to Marcus. Once in the bay, the sea state became calm and as they approached Monterey Peninsula Yacht Club marina, Yohana went to start the engine. The engine turned over but did not start. Yohana, looking at the fuel gauge, realized they were totally out of fuel, and cried out, "That bastard. I should have known he would do something rotten. He was on *Spirit* before I arrived and obviously did something so the fuel would slowly drain out while we were sailing."

"What we do now?" said Marcus.

"Well, this gets tricky," said Yohana. "I'll take the helm and Marcus, you take the mizzen. Juan, go forward and handle the main and jib. As we go past the breakwater into the marina, drop the sails on my command. If I time it right, the momentum of *Spirit* should drop to a crawl as we approach the dock. Luckily, we are outside the last slip. Juan, prepare to jump on the dock with the bow line. We should be going slow enough when we approach the dock. Cleat the line and I should be able to make *Spirit* pivot on the bow and swing around. Marcus, you get the boat hook ready to keep us from slamming into the dock when we swing around. If all goes well, we shouldn't damage *Spirit*."

As they secured the boat, Yohana grabbed Marcus, giving him a passionate kiss and saying, "Marcus you did an outstanding job. I really trust your capabilities. Next week I may have some interesting news for you. Have a good week. Say hi to Jenna and Sofia. I can't wait to see what they bought in the city."

Walking home Marcus had that strange feeling that he was being followed. Turning, he saw no one but to be on the safe side, he decided to circumnavigate the parking lot rather than walking through it leaving the marina dock gates. He took the coastal trail over to Washington Street, then up to Del Monte Ave. and over to Alvarado. Periodically he would stop and gaze in a store window trying to see if there was anyone behind. But there was no one. He finally chalked it up to anxiety on his part. As he approached the hotel, his thoughts then turned to *I wonder if next week she tells me what she's doing for her father. If so, I better talk to Station Chief Alonzo and get some guidance on how to respond. I'm sure he doesn't want me to blow my cover. This could get interesting.*

CHAPTER 15

A COMMON ADVERSARY

Yohana knew she would get a call from her father on Sunday and she couldn't wait. She was totally upset with the situation that occurred before sailing on Saturday.

At 2:30 her cell phone rang. Answering, she heard, "Yohana, listen…"

She immediately interrupted, saying, "Before you even speak, Father. I'm totally upset. You never listen to me or what's going on here. You only give me orders. Yesterday we had a very upsetting situation." She then related all that had happened on the Saturday sail and finished saying, "We are lucky that the weather and my capability prevailed. We could have lost *Spirit* had she crashed into the dock. Further, the new crew member I've been training is critical, as *Spirit* requires a crew of three on any of our operations and we are now never aware when Juan will get called to Pebble Beach. He has become a popular caddie. Now I don't know if I can trust Raul. I don't think I want to see him on the boat ever again."

Yohana's father was completely caught off guard with his daughter's outspoken candor. "Yohana, relax. Calm down. Raul is a key member of the family and one of the few that knows how to sail. I will speak to him."

"Speaking to him may not be enough. If he does anything to my new crew member, we can be in real jeopardy."

In a stern voice Yohana's father responded, saying, "Yohana, enough. There is a regatta in two weeks. You will enter. A shipment will be scheduled. I will give you details next week." And the phone went dead.

Closing her cell phone, Yohana's mind went into overdrive. *Well, I boxed myself in this time, telling my father I don't want Raul on the boat. I will need to use Marcus on this next operation. Can I trust him enough to tell him what we actually do? What excuse can I use to tell him we won't be coming back after the regatta. Jenna will think it's all about me getting close to Marcus. On the other hand, regardless of what my father says to Raul, he could show up at race time for the regatta. Juan is caddying today but I've got to chat with him to develop a plan.*

Yohana had Sunday night off so when Juan returned from Pebble Beach, she was waiting for him on their front porch. Juan no sooner parked his car and was walking up towards the house when there was a loud call in Spanish, "Juan, we have to talk. I got a call from Father and we have an operation but I think we also have an issue."

Juan came up on the porch and sat down next to Yohana, saying, "What's the problem? We've done this before." Yohana then explained to him what she had said to her father about Raul and her thoughts about what might happen. Juan responded with, "I think you can trust Marcus. He likes you and you like him, and I think a good relationship has developed between you both. So here's what I suggest we do. We don't tell Marcus about the operation, but do ask him to crew with us in the coming regatta. As I recall, it's Saturday so if we use Marcus on the operation, we would have him back on Sunday, so he wouldn't miss class the following week. But I suggest we don't tell Marcus about the operation until we set sail. That way he won't be able to compromise the operation because he'll be part of it. Now, if Raul shows up on Saturday to crew for the operation, we just apologize to Marcus and tell him there has been a change in plans and we are sorry but we won't need him for the regatta. We sail with Raul and Marcus never knows what we do."

⊕

Monday morning and the Petersons and Wongs were off to school. As they boarded the Presidio bus, Marcus thought he spotted Raul at the far side of the Transit Plaza. He didn't say anything to the others but his thoughts were *if that was Raul, I wonder if he's stalking me? I guess I better heed Yohana's warning. He could be dangerous and may want revenge.*

As they settled into their seats for the short bus ride to the Presidio, Jack Wong's first comment was, "You know, I really don't understand why we have to learn Malay. The one time I was in Singapore, everything was in English. All the signs were primarily in English as was most conversation with anybody. I don't think I ever heard Malay being spoken. Of course, I might not have recognized it had I heard it."

"That may be true," responded Marcus. "But I'm sure there are times when Malay is spoken between locals and if we are on a mission there, we have to be able to understand it and maybe even converse in it. After what we just went through learning Mandarin, I think this should be a breeze."

"I hope you're right."

"There is one other aspect. And I learned this in Italy on my last mission. It's not uncommon for locals to speak in multi-languages at the same time. The conversation can be in one primary language but words in other languages are injected when the speaker can't quite make the translation while speaking. That's really where being multilingual pays off."

⊕

They no sooner arrived in class when LiJing approached Marcus, saying, "My office at break time."

At break time the Wongs and Jenna went outside to eat their lunch while Marcus followed LiJing to her office where she related to him what she had heard from her father on the weekend. She said, "Marcus, a single Chinese software engineer from Beijing is scheduled to fly to Acapulco next week."

As she spoke, she passed a slip of paper to Marcus, saying, "Here is his name and description. I wrote it all down when we talked."

"Great, did he know whether he was military or CCP connected?"

"Sorry, he didn't have any of that info."

"This is all engrossing," said Marcus. "We have a regatta in two weeks and I expect Yohana will be asking me to crew for it. This could be the mission that we have been waiting for. But it's strange that it's only a single individual. Maybe it's just a precursor to a larger contingent being sent later."

"As originally planned, did he say whether he had passed this info on to CIA Station Chief Alonzo?"

"Yes, he did."

"Well, if so, I am sure I will be hearing from him with some sort of marching orders. Thanks again. We better get back to class."

⟨Ⅱ⟩

Coincidentally as class began in the afternoon, LiJing opened with a similar statement as what Marcus had told Jack on the bus. But she further added that in Singapore there are newspapers published in both Malay, Mandarin and English, and currently there is a daily in Malay and a daily in Mandarin, among the other English newspapers being published.

⟨Ⅱ⟩

As anticipated, Marcus's cell phone rang at 5:30 the next morning, waking both he and Jenna up. Before answering, he said, "Based on what we learned from LiJing yesterday and considering it's 8:30 in New York, I'm sure it's Station Chief Alonzo."

Jenna rolled over to go back to sleep while Marcus fumbled on the side table looking for his cell phone as it rang loudly again. "Marcus, answer it." yelled Jenna, continuing with, "You have to change your cell phone ring. That 'old phone' ring tone is just too loud."

Picking up his phone, Marcus answered, "Agent Peterson here."

"Station Chief Alonzo here. Agent Peterson, it appears there may be a Chinese import about to occur. Are any regattas scheduled?"

"Yes, sir. There is one scheduled in two weeks. Yohana will probably enter *Spirit*. She enters all regattas. If a shipment is scheduled, I'm sure she will not return with the other boats at the completion of the regatta but will sail out to sea to meet as per her usual. Both Coast Guard ships will probably remain in the bay keeping noncompeting boats away from the regatta course, not monitoring whose entering or leaving the bay."

"This could be great if you could crew with her. I suggest you maintain your undercover status. If she invites you to be crew, she will obviously have to confide in you what's going on. If she does, you should maintain your friendship with her, assuring her that you won't report anything to the authorities. Your interest is only sailing. This is all predicated on what kind of friendship you've been able to develop with her."

"That may be a possibility. I'll certainly give it a try. Usually on operations, in addition to her brother, another member of La eMe, the local Mexican Mafia family her father heads, sails with her. I witnessed an altercation she had with him the other day, which could open a window for me to participate. In a somewhat protective mode, I participated in the altercation not realizing who he was. Though alienating him, I think it strengthened my relationship with her."

"Keep Agent Rodriguez informed with any interfaces you have with the local La eMe. They are the local FBI's issue, not ours."

Marcus finished the call with Station Chief Alonzo and brought Jenna up to speed with what he was told, further explaining to her that if he did participate in an operation, he would obviously not be coming home after the regatta and had no idea when he would return. He would certainly keep her apprised by cell phone if able. This obviously didn't go over well with Jenna, as she still felt Yohana was a threat to their marriage.

⚓

Saturday morning of race day, Juan and Yohana were on their way to the marina. As planned, they had already invited Marcus to crew with them in the regatta. "Now Yohana, remember our plan. If Raul shows up, you just tell him there has been a change in plans," said Juan.

"Got it," said Yohana.

Reaching the marina they started getting their gear out of the car and were about to head to *Spirit* when Juan's cell phone went off. "This could be a problem," he said opening his cell and answering, "Juan Mendez here. Yes, sir. I understand. I'll be on my way. I should be there before 10." Hanging up and turning to Yohana, he said, "We've got a problem. That was work. Their top Pro has a tee time at 10 with some special guest and is insisting on me caddying."

"What do we do?" asked Yohana.

"Well, if both Raul and Marcus show, at least you have a crew. Though the operation could be gripping. Marcus will learn all and will be part of it. If Raul doesn't show, I'm sure you can recruit one of the college sailors that are always there at regatta time looking for a crew slot. You will have to figure out how to drop him or her off before you leave the Bay after the regatta. You could handle the operation with just Marcus as you're motoring most of the time."

For an instant Yohana's mind went into spin, thinking, *With Marcus with me I can handle anything.* And turning to Juan with a serious stern face, she said, "Juan, take the car. I've got this."

CHAPTER 16

THE OPERATION

A s Yohana approached the dock, she was happy to see that Marcus had already arrived and was unpacking and installing the sails on *Spirit*. She also saw Raul coming from the other end of the parking lot.

Quickly getting onboard, she grabbed Marcus, whispering in his ear, "I like you, Marcus, but this is for Raul." Just as Raul approached the boat, she put her arms around Marcus, giving him a very passionate kiss. Then calling to Raul in Spanish, she said, "Raul, Juan had to work today so I recruited my boyfriend, Marcus. He is a good sailor; in fact, he could be a skipper. If and when I turn the helm over to him, I expect complete cooperation." Then as Raul boarded, in English she said in a very authoritative voice to both of them, "I don't care what happened the last time you saw each other. I expect you both to work together during the regatta and after. Understand?"

They both agreed and immediately went to work setting the sails on *Spirit* but with different thoughts in their minds. Raul's: *Well, my friend Marcus, if that's what they call you, before this trip ends you will die.* Marcus's: *This Raul must be part of the Mafia family. We are obviously going on the operation.*

⊕

They did well in the race and Yohana gave control to Marcus several times during the race. Yohana was at the helm as they rounded the last mark and instead of setting a course to the marina, she headed out of the bay to the ocean.

Marcus was at mid-deck at the time and called out, "Yohana, where are you going?"

"I'm sorry, Marcus," she responded. "We have another activity that we must take care of. I think we're close enough to old Monterey for cell service. You might want to call Jenna and let her know you're going to be quite late getting back. Definitely after dark. Maybe in the morning."

Raul had been below deck and coming into the cockpit heard their conversation and said in Spanish, "Yohana, doesn't Marcus know what we're doing?"

Yohana, responding in Spanish, said, "No, but he will soon find out. According to my father, we are only supposed to pick up one Chinese and drop him off close to Santa Cruz. They will be sending a boat out to meet us, so we won't have to enter Santa Cruz Marina. In fact, they may meet us before we even get to Santa Cruz. They have our call numbers and will be radioing us. Now stay cool with this. I'll do the explaining with Marcus as necessary."

⊕

The ocean was quite calm; the wind had died down to a breeze and they were several miles out when Yohana put *Spirit* into the wind, started the engine and called out, "Drop the sails. Raul, go in the pilothouse and man the GPS console. Guide me to the designated position. Marcus, secure the sails. If the wind comes up later, we may sail again."

It was early evening but still light. They had been holding the position for less than an hour when Raul called up from below saying, "You should be able to see them. They just called on the radio."

Yohana picked up the binoculars and looked south, saying, "I see them now. Come up on deck, Raul. Both you and Marcus, put the bumpers out on the starboard side. Raul, take the bow, Marcus take the stern. They will have lines to secure them to us."

The whole operation took just minutes. The sleek Picuda smuggling boat approached, was secured, Spanish conversation occurred between Yohana and the skipper of the Picuda, the Chinese passenger with a small bag came aboard *Spirit*. The Picuda's lines were released and it started south at high speed. Yohana motioned to the passenger to sit and asked, "Understand English?"

In somewhat stilted English the passenger said, "Yes. my name is Duyi Chang, from Beijing, China. Do we go to Avocado Company?"

Yohana responded, "Yes. I'll explain in a minute." Then looking up she called out, "Raul, put up the jib for stability. Marcus, come to the cockpit." Starting the engine and heading toward the Bay entrance, she then looked back at the passenger, saying, "Marcus will take you below. We will motor into Monterey Bay where we will meet a boat from Avocado Company that will take you to shore."

As Marcus stepped into the cockpit, he startled both Yohana and the passenger by saying in perfect Mandarin, "Welcome to the USA. I will show you below. It should be an easy trip in but you will be more comfortable out of the wind."

The startled passenger held out his hand to shake and responded in Mandarin, saying, "Thank you. Are you from the Avocado Company?"

"No. I only crew for the woman captain. Please follow me," said Marcus. Then looking up at Yohana, he said in English, "Yohana, I've been studying the Chinese language at the Presidio. I'll take him below and chat with him to make him feel comfortable. Is that okay?"

"Great," responded Yohana while her mind went into overdrive. *Marcus is acting like he's been a part of this operation all along. Does he really know what's going on? I don't know whether this is good or bad.*

⊕

In a relatively calm sea the transfer of the Chinese passenger to the Avocado Company cabin cruiser, a Bayliner 35, went easy and quickly. *Spirit* was met by the Bayliner in the middle of Monterey Bay about halfway between Santa Cruz and Monterey.

After the transfer, both yachts headed in opposite directions. The Bayliner headed north to Santa Cruz while Yohana put *Spirit* on course headed south directly to the Monterey Marina.

Turning to Marcus she said, "Marcus, take the helm and just keep her on this course. Raul and I will go below deck and rustle up some food. We have several hours ahead of us to get home so nourishment is definitely in order."

With that said, she and Raul immediately entered the pilothouse and went below chatting loudly in Spanish to each other. "Yohana, we have to waste Marcus before we get in cell range of Monterey. Now that he knows what we do, he could blow the whole thing by reporting us to the authorities. We can't let that happen."

"Raul, are you out of your mind? You can't just kill him. What would we tell everybody when we returned? I trust him. He's not going to report us. He likes me too much."

"Yohana, you're naïve. I'm sure he's the guy that was with that blonde that accosted me the night we were unloading the drugs from *Spirit*. We've got to get rid of him. He could have a sailing accident, falling overboard and drowning. In the dark we could not see to save him."

"Raul, cease! He's not going to report us, and the fact that he can converse in Chinese makes him an asset to have along when we transfer the group that's expected. Besides, I don't want to be involved in any murder. Now, we've got a great meal in the cooler that the chef at the Sardine Factory made for me. Let's get it out and serve it up. I'm starved."

Raul didn't say another word out loud but to himself, he thought, *I'm sorry Yohana, I can't take the risk. If the opportunity presents itself, he's going to die.*

⊕

Shortly after they had eaten, a light wind came up. Yohana cut the engine and had Marcus and Raul raise the sails. The direction they were going put them on a port tack as soon as the sails filled. Yohana called out, "Marcus, come take the helm. If you pinch a little more to a close reach and the wind holds this direction, we will be on a direct course to the marina. Raul, go below and get some shut-eye. We will take the first watch. I'll wake you in an hour or so."

It was a beautiful night to sail: a full moon, a calm sea, and the soft sound of the water hissing on the hull as *Spirit* glided through the water. Yohana settled in next to Marcus in the fantail with a serape draped over their legs for warmth. Marcus had one arm around her and the other stretched forward holding the wheel. His thoughts, *This is like a magical dream. Sailing an awesome yacht with a beautiful woman in my arms. How pleasurable can it get?*

⟐

They had been sailing about an hour and a half. Yohana was asleep. Marcus was somewhat mesmerized staring at the binnacle light and periodically checking the sails.

They were still on a close reach to port and the moderate wind gave them speed close to 7 knots. He hadn't heard or noticed Raul approaching on the main deck in front of the pilothouse holding a beretta with a silencer pointed directly at him.

The main fluttered a little in a wind gust, causing Marcus to look up. In a matter of seconds, he spotted Raul and spun the wheel causing *Spirit* to come about to a starboard tack. The mainsail's boom caught Raul at the waist as it swung across the deck to the starboard side, sending him flying. The gun he was holding went off, firing a bullet up in the air and then dropped as he clawed the air screaming, "Noooooooooo," before he hit the water.

Yohana woke up and as an avid sailor, instinctively grabbed one of the "man overboard" units secured in the cockpit and threw it out on the starboard side. Taking the wheel from Marcus, and putting *Spirit* into the wind, she called, "Marcus, go drop the main and mizzen."

Starting the engine and as the sheets came down, she turned *Spirit* back in the direction they had come from. By the time this was accomplished, they were considerably south from where Raul was knocked off the boat. As Marcus came back to the cockpit, Yohana said, "Look for the blinking light of the 'man overboard' unit. Hopefully Raul was able to swim to the life preserver attached to it."

"Yohana, that bastard was about to shoot me. Why are we trying to save him?" said Marcus.

"Well, he is not going to shoot you now. His gun is lying on the deck next to the handrail. He obviously dropped it when he was hit by the main boom. Better get it before it drops overboard. We will deal with his threat after we keep him from drowning."

Marcus went out and picked up the gun and brought it back to the cockpit. "This is quite a gun. I have never seen a Beretta fitted with a silencer before. I'll put it down below later, but I think I spotted a flashing light slightly starboard. Let me check it out," said Marcus as he picked up the binoculars for a better look. "There appears to be other lights on the port side further out. Who would be sailing at this hour?"

"That's probably the fishing fleet from Santa Cruz. They would be going out about this time," said Yohana.

"We are still too far away to be sure that's the "man overboard" unit that's flashing, but set a course for it and I'll keep watching it when I come back up," said Marcus as he went below with the pistol.

Marcus was able to determine that the beacon was from the "man overboard" unit as they got closer, but couldn't determine much else as the beacon didn't put much light on the life preserver that was attached. As they came up on the unit, Yohana screamed, "Oh no. There is no one there. Raul didn't get to the life preserver. He must have drowned. Oh, what am I going to do?"

"Calm yourself, Yohana. It was an accident. Not your fault," said Marcus as he lifted the unit out of the water and stowed it back in its place in the cockpit.

"Marcus, you don't understand," said Yohana.

"There is nothing more we can do here, Yohana. Let's go home," responded Marcus. Yohana turned *Spirit* around setting into the wind as Marcus went forward and raised the main and mizzen. As the sails went up and caught the wind, Yohana brought *Spirit* into a close port reach, putting them back on a heading toward Old Monterey marina.

"Marcus, you don't understand. I'm totally afraid of my father, of you, of what will happen, of everything," said Yohana to Marcus as he got back in the cockpit. Sensing she was totally upset, his thoughts were, *I have got to calm her down. Make her feel there is no problem here with me or the operation. I'm not sure what I can say about Raul.*

"Yohana, listen. I had a long talk with the Chinese engineer we picked up and transferred to the Avocado boat. He is a key department head in the Avocado division in China. He explained that due to the current international conditions, this was the only way the company could move employees around. I have no problem with that. The Avocado Corporation is one of the largest technology companies in the United States. And one of the richest. I'm sure they know what they're doing. He told me about the group that is supposed to follow him and would be coming in the same way as he did. I'll be more than happy to help you on that operation. You won't need Raul. We just have to make sure Juan doesn't have to work. I suspected that your father was involved, but understand. Technically, you did nothing illegal. You merely transferred people from one boat to another. The Avocado boat executed the illegal entry of the Chinese engineer to the US."

"Oh, thank you, Marcus. I feel a little better, but I don't know what to say to my father if he asks about Raul. Raul is a key member of my father's organization, and somehow Raul gets word to him about every operation he is part of. I don't know how he does it, as I can't even call my father. My only communication with him is when he calls me, and it's always from some different number. Since cell phones are not allowed in prison, someone must get him one when he needs to make a call."

"Yohana, pure and simple, you can honestly tell him it was an accident. We did everything we could to save him. Look, I'll take the helm, go down below and get some rest or make us some coffee. We have a ways to go. We probably won't get to the marina before dawn."

CHAPTER 17

RECKONING

I t was dawn as *Spirit* pulled into the Monterey Marina. Having been called by Yohana on her cell, Juan was on the wharf ready to meet it.

"Welcome home," called Juan. "Throw me a bow line, Marcus. Yohana, cut the engine. You should be able to pivot into the dock when I secure the bow. Marcus, put a bumper out starboard and get ready to throw me a line from the stern."

"Well, you're in ordering mood this morning." called back Yohana.

"Just doing my job, assisting in the docking of *Spirit*," responded Juan with a smile.

As they finished securing *Spirit*, Yohana said, "Marcus, get your gear, go home and get some rest. I'll brief Juan as we stow the sails and lock up *Spirit*. Maybe we could meet at the club tonight. My treat. You were excellent as crew."

"Thanks, Yohana. That would be great. I'm on my way. I suggest you or Juan should stow that gun away some place. I left it down below on the chart table. See you later tonight at the club."

☮

All was quiet in the condo as Marcus entered. Jenna was still sound asleep. Quietly undressing, he slipped under the covers of the bed. Jenna never moved, obviously still in a deep sleep. In a matter of minutes, Marcus joined her.

Shortly after, the sun, streaming in their bedroom window along with the loud snoring of Marcus, woke Jenna up. Seeing that Marcus was still sound asleep, she decided to get up and quietly get dressed. She and the Wongs had agreed to meet at Abalonetti's Bar and Grill for brunch at 11:00 and it was getting close to that time. *I don't know when he got in but he is sleeping so soundly, I'll just leave a note and go meet the Wongs,* she thought.

℗

It was noon when Marcus finally woke up. A note from Jenna on the bedside table said she was out for brunch with the Wongs and to call when he got up. *I could sleep another hour or so,* he thought, *but I'm also pretty hungry. It's got to be brunch.* A quick call, shower, short walk and Marcus walked into Abalonetti's. Upon seeing him, the small group sitting at the only occupied table raised their glasses and said, "Welcome home, Marcus."

This was followed with Jack saying, "Come join us. We are dying to hear about your adventure. Your quick call to Jenna last night describing what was happening gave us all a little concern. But you're alive and well and here, so come and fill us in. I've ordered you a mimosa to lubricate your tongue."

Marcus sat down, sipped his mimosa, ordered his brunch and began relating his story. The reaction around the table was varied. None of them being sailboat racing enthusiasts, they were not enthused by his description of the regatta and the sailing achievements they were able to accomplish with *Spirit* and the comments generated only polite interested expressions. The relating of Raul becoming part of the crew achieved a concerned look on Jenna's face, but she said nothing.

His description of the pickup and delivering of Duyi Chang to the Avocado company boat and what he learned from his discussion with the Avocado engineer immediately sparked an excited expression on Jenna's face as she said, "Oh, great. You got all the information that Station Chief Alonzo wanted. You don't have to be under cover anymore and sail with Yohana."

"Well, that's not totally true," responded Marcus. "I did commit to Yohana that I would crew for her in the next regatta and I'm sure, since the next Chinese shipment, so to speak, will include students, Alonzo will be interested in what universities are a part of this transfer. But let me continue." His recount of the trip home, the murder attempt and possible drowning of Raul caused deep concern by all and intense questioning. This was cut off when Marcus said, "What will be, will be. We can't speculate further. Let's enjoy our brunch. Oh, by the way, Yohana has invited us, you and I", he said pointing to Jenna, "to dinner tonight at the club, something of an appreciation gesture for my performance as crew."

⊕

On the walk home to the condo, Jenna's cell phone went off. "Who could that be on Sunday afternoon?" she said as she flipped open her phone.

Seeing the screen and recognizing the name she answered, "Hi, Fred. Haven't talked to you in quite a while. What's the issue? I'm with Marcus and we are on our way home. I'll put you on speaker."

"Hi Jenna, I'm afraid it's not a social call and you probably aren't interested in hearing this; however, remember Adriana Gambioni didn't get arrested in California and quietly returned to New York. The others involved in your kidnapping were arrested and are currently serving time in a California prison. Well, Nunzio Gambioni, her brother-in-law, was killed during an internal prison rumble. Adriana considers you are the cause and is trying to reestablish another effort by members of the crime family to take you out. With Franco and Nunzio both dead, I'm not sure she has much clout in the family anymore. Currently there is nothing we can arrest her for but our sources will keep us apprised of any activity. I felt it important to make you aware."

"What wonderful news for Sunday afternoon," facetiously responded Jenna. "Currently out here we're not sure whether we are in or out with the local Mexican Mafia. I'll let Marcus fill you in."

Marcus related a brief rundown of the regatta activity and Fred responded, "I would make sure you brief Agent Rodriguez. He is better able to anticipate what to expect the local Mafia will do relative to Raul. They function entirely differently than the Italian Mafia here, especially when some of their leadership is incarcerated. If they are anything like the cartel in Mexico, they can be very treacherous. I'm sure Agent Rodriguez will be able to advise you."

☾

The Peterson household was awakened at 5 AM by both the alarm clock on Marcus's bedside table and the phone on Jenna's bedside table. Both went off simultaneously. It was not unanticipated. A conference call with the CIA office in New York had been arranged the afternoon before and their start time was 8 AM.

Marcus turned off the alarm and rolled over, saying to Jenna, "That will be Station Chief Alonzo. You answer it, Jenna. I'll go get on the extension in the living room."

Marcus grabbed his robe and ran into the condo living room while Jenna picked up the phone saying, "Good morning, Station Chief Alonzo. Marcus will be with you shortly. Is Agent Rodriguez on the line?"

"He will be shortly, Jenna. My secretary is getting him now."

"Agent Peterson here," said Marcus as he picked up the other extension.

"Good morning Marcus." said Station Chief Alonzo. "Please proceed with the briefing."

Marcus went through the entire event in detail, describing all that happened on the regatta, the transfer of the Chinese engineer to the Avocado motor launch and the information he had received from the Chinese engineer.

Jenna was listening to the whole conversation on the bedroom extension and became very upset when she heard Station Chief Alonzo saying, "Marcus, I want you to continue developing a close relationship with Yohana. Being part of the next operation involving the smuggling of Chinese into the country is critical. We must learn what universities are involved and whether any of the Chinese are military or connected to the CCP. Hopefully you will be able to get this information by conversing with them while they are on *Spirit*. Agent Rodriguez, work with Marcus on the Raul issue. We can't let that compromise the overall objective." The call ended with Agent Rodriguez assuring that he would follow up on the Raul issue if it became a problem.

Hanging up the phone and sensing that Jenna's jealousy had probably gone into high gear with what she had just heard, Marcus went to her and took her in his arms, giving her a passionate kiss before she could say anything. Then as he held her, he said, "Look, Jenna, I know you're upset about the Yohana relationship but let me assure you I'm totally attracted to you, no one else, and I love you dearly." As Marcus spoke, he began to lightly brush his fingers along her arm, her cheek, her neck, and running downward along the curve of her waist and her hips and slipping his hand inside her t-shirt night gown. He spoke quietly, "Yes, initially Yohana was quite flirtatious; however, the relationship has become very platonic. I consider her and treat her no different than my sister. Last night when we were at the club having dinner with them, it was more or less like just being with family."

Jenna turned to him and began to respond to his touch and helping him off with his housecoat, she said, "You may think that, Marcus, but let me be clear. She definitely has eyes on you. You may see and emotionally feel what you want, but I see and feel what is real." Marcus continued to gently caress her, brushing his hand along the skin below her navel and then stroking back up around the curves of her breasts and along her ribs. She responded by pulling his head to her breasts but saying, "I may not like your assignment but it's your job and I will try to deal with it." They then made love several times, communicating further with each other the entire time by only their eyes and touch. Wary fears seemed to slip from Jenna's mind.

⟨⟩

The second alarm that Jenna had set went off at seven, awakening them both. "We have got to hustle, Marcus. We don't want to miss the bus to the Presidio," said Jenna. "This week we are in total immersion with Malay. I don't know about you, but I'm having a lot more difficulty with this language than I did with Mandarin."

"I am having a little difficulty myself. I am going to suggest to LiJing that since we meet for dinner a couple of times a week at the club, maybe we could try utilizing the language between ourselves while we are there. Using it in a different environment other than the classroom might help," said Marcus. "Let's chat with the Wongs on the bus on the way in this morning, see if they're having the same problem. Hopefully, we can concentrate on our class work for the next few weeks. There'll be no sailing until the next regatta, and if Fred can keep the possible Gambioni issue under control in New York, we should be good to go."

After the brief chat they leaped out of bed, showered, dressed, and ran for the bus. A brief stop at the breakfast room in the hotel on the way provided coffee and doughnuts to go.

CHAPTER 18

THE PAST BECKONS

I t had been a demanding week for the Petersons and it was only Thursday. One more school day to go. There had been no time for relaxation: class all day, study all night. The walk home from the Presidio bus stop was in total silence. Little did they know they were about to get a fateful call.

The house phone in the condo was ringing as they entered. "Who could be calling on the condo phone? And at this time of day," said Marcus as he picked up the receiver, answering, "Hello, Peterson residence. Oh, Dad. Hi. How are you?"

"Not good, son. It's your sister. She's missing. We think she's been kidnapped. She called when she left work Tuesday saying she was coming home and we haven't seen or heard from her since. She doesn't answer her cell phone and we've checked with all her friends and no one else has seen or heard from her."

"Have you called the police?"

"Yes, we filed a missing persons with the police today. Also, we received a card in the mail today. No return address and all it said was 'you deserve this'."

Marcus could hear his mother sobbing in the background. He continued, "Dad, try to calm Mom. I'll be there as soon as I can; I will call you back in a few minutes." Hanging up the phone and turning to Jenna, he said, "My sister's been kidnapped and from a note my folks got, it appears to be the Gambioni family."

"Marcus, call Fred right away. I'll get you a flight reservation," said Jenna.

Marcus grabbed his cell and dialed their FBI friend Fred, who answered on the second ring saying, "I know, Marcus. It's your sister. We've got this. We heard from our sources that the new head of the organization would have nothing to do with any killing when Adriana asked them to go about taking you both out again. However, he did agree to kidnapping your sister and delivering her to Adriana. We almost stopped it before it began, but we were not quick enough. We know your sister is safe and we know where she is. We plan to get her, Adriana, and anyone else that's involved during the transfer."

"Thanks, Fred. I'll tell my folks. Jenna's getting me a flight home. I'll call you in the morning when I arrive."

⟨D⟩

Astrid Peterson had no idea what happened. She remembered leaving her office, calling her folks and telling them she was on her way home, and taking the elevator down and walking out the front door of the office building she worked in. Someone was approaching her on the crowded sidewalk and she remembered feeling a tap on her back, then nothing.

As she woke up, she found herself lying on a long needlepoint embroidered davenport that was covered in plastic, in what appeared to be a small sitting room. There was an upholstered chair across from her and a coffee table with a bottle of water in front of her. As she went to get up, she grabbed her head and cried out, "Ow." *Where am I?* she thought. *How did I get here? Why is my head pounding?* She slowly got up, balancing herself by holding onto one arm of the couch. She was about to walk towards the door but was startled as the door to the room opened and two masked strangers, speaking Italian to each other, walked in, an older woman and a young man.

Seeing Astrid standing, the older woman motioned for her to sit down and said, "I'm sorry, honey. We had to keep you sedated and I'm sure the chloroform gave you that throbbing head. Don't be alarmed, you're safe and you won't be here very long. That's all I can tell you. Now drink some water and lay back down. That will help clear your head."

Astrid, totally upset, tears forming in her eyes, sat back down on the couch and reaching for the water said an unsettled voice, "What's going on? Where am I? Why am I here? Who are you?"

⊕

As Marcus's plane taxied to the gate at LaGuardia airport in New York, and in anticipation of calling Fred, he switched his phone off airplane mode.

It immediately rang and looking at the screen, he saw it was from a number he did not know. He clicked to answer but before he could, a voice said, "Welcome home, Marcus. I'm glad you didn't change your cell phone number. I've been trying to call you all morning. I knew I could get you back to New York and I knew you'd be arriving sometime this morning. Now you can prepare to join Franco." The phone then went dead.

Marcus immediately called Fred, who answered on the first ring, "Welcome home, Marcus. How was the flight?"

"The flight was fine but I just got a call from someone whom I'm sure was Adriana threatening my death."

"Well now, that makes sense. She couldn't get the crime family to take you out but she could get them to do a kidnapping that would bring you back. She probably then figured for a price she could get an individual to take you out. We know where they're holding your sister and we will move out on that. Now, she doesn't know where you are or what flight you came in on, so the move on you is probably planned to occur when you arrive at home. My guess is it could be a drive-by."

"What are we to do?" said Marcus.

"Due to normal traffic in and out of the airport, they won't be expecting you right away. We have an armored SUV painted like a cab that we use in some of our operations and it's located fairly close to the airport. I'll have that pick you up. It's painted yellow and has a number 27 on it. They'll call your cell when they're approaching your terminal. We will also move out on Adriana as she will definitely be remote from anything she planned. You be watchful. I'll see you soon."

⊕

As predicted, the yellow SUV arrived at the terminal and Marcus got right in. The driver immediately said, "Sit back and relax. You are totally safe in here. This vehicle has the same armor as the President's limousine."

The ride in from the airport was smooth but as soon as the cab entered the street that the Petersons' house was on everything began happening fast. They no sooner slowed down in front of Marcus's parents' house when out of nowhere a black Town Car drove up, slowed down and automatic weapons appeared out the windows riddling the cab with automatic fire. At the same time, black and whites appeared driving towards the scene from both ends of the street. The Town Car was stopped and a shootout between its occupants and the police ensued. After the shooting stopped, Marcus exited the SUV unscathed and went into his parents' home. Shortly after there was a knock on the door and Fred appeared with his sister.

Marcus hugged her, saying, "Astrid, I'm so glad you're alright. I'm so sorry this happened." Then looking at Fred, he asked, "What's the status?"

"The two gunmen were killed in the shootout and the driver arrested. Adriana has also been arrested for kidnapping and conspiracy to commit murder. I think the Gambioni issue is finally put to bed. I've spoken to Station Chief Alonzo and he wishes to see you this afternoon. He indicated reservations have been made for you to return to California tomorrow morning. He'll give you the flight details when you see him. I have to get back to the station and take care of the paperwork. Have a good trip back; say hi to Jenna for me. Oh, you better explain to your sister and parents why all this happened. See you."

"Thanks so much," said Marcus as he ushered Fred out the door.

⌖

Dinner at the Petersons' was a family affair. They sat down at the table to a meal of Marcus's favorites prepared by his mother: sma kottbullar (Swedish meatballs) with sauce for dinner and plattar (Swedish pancakes) with lingonberry spread for dessert. A laptop at the end of the table allowed Jenna to join the party via Zoom.

Marcus's parents were totally unaware of the cases he and Jenna had been on and the involvement of the Gambioni Mafia crime family. They became mesmerized as Marcus and Jenna explained what led up to the day's activities. After discussing the events of the day, the conversation went on to the pleasurable things that Marcus and Jenna had been doing in California, which lightened the whole evening up.

CHAPTER 19

RAUL

R aul was a little nervous about going to the state prison, but he had been summoned by the local capo to visit and report. He had been told to dress formally and present himself as a defense attorney. He should request a client council visit with Carlos Mendez, currently being held on drug charges. Credentials had been prepared for him by one of the other members of the La eMe family.

The visiting area for client and lawyer consisted of individual tables for two strategically spaced apart. Inmates were brought in with chains on ankles and wrists, the ankles fastened to the tables. Carlos Mendez was already seated when Raul was brought in. There were several guards stationed around the room and other inmates talking to their lawyers at different tables.

Raul carried a briefcase that was searched when he arrived and took out some legal papers, laying them on the table in front of Carlos. He then proceeded to converse with Carlos in Spanish and started by reporting the altercation he had with Yohana and Marcus at his arrival at *Spirit* before the regatta started. Specifically saying, "Carlos, I'm sure that

Marcus was part of the couple that accosted me when we were unloading the drugs. Yohana, however, thinks he's the greatest and is in love with him. She thinks he can be trusted and will do anything for her. I told her that was bull shit but agreed to sail with him."

"Enough of that, Raul, tell me about the operation."

"Well, after the regatta, which we did well in, we went out and met the cartel's Picuda and transferred a Chinese engineer. We delivered him to an Avocado motor launch in the middle of Monterey Bay and then started the sail home. Prior to the transfer operation, Marcus was below deck with the Chinese engineer talking Chinese. After the transfer, the bay was flat and we had a slight breeze in the right direction so we raised the sails and started an easy reach back to Monterey. After about an hour, Yohanna was asleep next to Marcus at the helm. I had brought along my pistol with a silencer and I quietly went up on deck to take Marcus out."

"You what?" shot back Carlos. "Raul, when the hell are you going learn to take orders? I specifically told you not to harm him. I had promised Yohana you wouldn't."

"Well, I didn't. Marcus quickly came about before I could get a shot off and the main boom came across and knocked me overboard. Luckily, I yelled and Yohana woke up and automatically threw one of the life preserver kits overboard. I was able to swim to it but being under sail, *Spirit* was long gone. I don't know if they ever turned around and came looking for me. It was shortly before dawn and the fishing fleet out of Santa Cruz was heading out. One of the boats saw me, pulled me out of the water and eventually I got home. The fishing boat left that survival kit in the water so if they ever came back for me, they probably thought I drowned. Did Yohana say anything to you about it when she reported about the operation?"

"No, she just talked about the Chinese transfer but never mentioned the trip home. She was probably afraid I'd chew her out for drowning you."

"Would you have?"

"Quite frankly, no. If she described what you just told me, I would've told her you deserved it for disobeying my orders. Now don't get upset as I'm going to give you a new assignment. In the current operation we sell the drugs we receive from the Mexican cartel and split the revenue with them. In this new operation, the Chinese are contracting with the cartel to provide transportation to the US of their personnel. I have negotiated with them on what our piece of the action is. I want you to go down to Acapulco to set up an account in the Bank of Mexico there to receive those funds. I wouldn't get too concerned as you should to be able to fly down there without any problem. You were born here and have a passport. While you are there, the cartel will take good care of you. Without us, they don't get their final payment from the Chinese until they are assured that their personnel have arrived."

"When do I have to be there?"

"I've already told the capo of the cartel and the Bank of Mexico that you will be there the day after tomorrow. So I would get your ass in gear and get your airline reservation as soon as you leave here. Now let's finish up our little charade here by both of us signing these papers that I've been pretending to read while we've been talking." Raul carefully put the papers back in his briefcase and signaled the guards that he was ready to leave. Two immediately approached the table to escort him out and take Carlos back to his cell. As he got up and turned to leave, he was a little taken back by Carlos's comment in English, "Make that ticket one-way."

CHAPTER 20

THE WORD FROM
SINGAPORE

C lass at the Presidio was getting complex as they closed in on the
course's primary objective: the development of a comfortable feeling when living in a multiple language society such as Singapore. There,
a social or business gathering in the predominant conversational language of English may be sprinkled with words and phrases of Malay
and/or Mandarin.

Having completed an extensive study of Mandarin, the current class
study was of the Malay language. However, in class LiJing led all discussions in a mixture of Mandarin, Malay, and English and the class was
encouraged to respond accordingly. In addition, LiJing had subscriptions
to two Singapore newspapers, one published in Malay and one published
in Mandarin. They were available for the class to read and utilized for
class discussions. It was in one of these periodicals published in Mandarin that Marcus discovered an unusual advertisement. It indicated that
applications for graduate fellowships on selected scientific research

projects at prominent US East-Coast colleges were being accepted. It gave only a local Singapore phone number. Class discussions came up with the possibility that either the Chinese military or the CCP was recruiting potential spies. After class Marcus asked LiJing if she would question her dad in Singapore the next time she spoke to him.

⟐

Shortly after class LiJing sent an email to her dad in Singapore asking for a classified call and also mentioning the newspaper article. Being that it was early morning in Singapore he was up and happened to be on his computer. He immediately responded that he had planned to set up a call to her also as he had some information that should be passed on and he could be at the US Consulate the following morning at 9 o'clock and she should place the call on the Presidio secure line to the same number he had given her before. He further indicated he would look into the newspaper article today and maybe be able to have information concerning it.

⟐

The following day LiJing dismissed her class early. Catching Jenna as the students were filing out, she said, "Jenna, I'll be talking to my dad later today and if he has any information for you, I will call you or Marcus on your cell phones."

"Thanks, LiJing, we will be home all night," answered Jenna.

LiJing then went to her office to make the call to her dad on a Presidio secure line to the US Consulate in Singapore. The routing of the call again took several minutes but eventually she heard her father's voice greeting her. "Hi, Father," she responded. "You said you had some information for my CIA students."

"Yes, it could pertain to the next group of Chinese to be smuggled into the US. I had dinner with Jack Yang, my travel agent friend, the other night, and he apprised me of the latest travel arrangements he made for the Chinese. It was a group of eight. Seven needed flights to Acapulco, Mexico (again one-way) and one needed flights to Boston, Mass. (also one-way). He said that they appeared to be quite excited about going to the US and came to his office as a group and were very talkative. Four of them were software engineers from Beijing and four engineering students. And that's the interesting part. Two of the engineering students were graduates of Beijing Institute of Technology and two were graduates of our local Singapore Polytechnic. Of the two locals, one was from here in Singapore and the other was his cousin from Beijing. All four students were quite excited because they had received a graduate fellowship at a US university."

"Did he know how the one going to Boston got a student visa?" asked LiJing.

"Yes. He said the student told him it was easy. He just went to the US Consulate with his university acceptance letter and his Singapore passport, and there was no problem getting the visa. I suggest you pass this information on to CIA Station Chief Alonzo. I believe you have a secure link from the consulate to the CIA office in New York."

"Yes, I intend to do so."

"Oh, were you able to do any follow-up on the newspaper advertisement?" asked LiJing.

"I'm afraid not. The follow-up phone number was disconnected. That's not uncommon. People who run an ad with a follow-up phone number usually cancel the phone number after they have received the replies they are looking for."

"Thanks much, Father. I will pass this on."

CHAPTER 21

PREPARATION

The last regatta of the season and the anticipated major smuggling operation was a week away. The second exam, again an escape room test, had been completed and Jenna and Jack's team had escaped first. Knowing that Marcus would be helping Juan and Yohana with getting *Spirit* ready for next week's regatta, Jack had agreed to take Jenna and Sophia up to the city for a shopping tour as a sort of prize for completing the test.

In this escape room test all written clues and conversation was in Malay, making it quite a challenge for all. When Marcus arrived at the Marina, he was surprised to find only Yohana aboard *Spirit* and dressed in sweats, which she rarely wore when sailing.

"Yohana, where's Juan? Are we not taking *Spirit* out today?" asked Marcus.

"He's at Pebble Beach again. An important pro wanted him to caddy. But he will be available tomorrow, so we will be able to take her out for a practice sail. I was going to call you to let you know we wouldn't be sailing till tomorrow but with Juan gone, I do need a little help today," responded Yohana.

"When tomorrow? I'm not sure I can make it. We have other plans," responded Marcus.

"It will be in the afternoon as Juan has another caddy date in the early morning. Probably around 1 o'clock. There should be a breeze about then and our main accomplishment should be practicing setting and downing the spinnaker. Hopefully we should be able to make two goes at it. I too have to work Sunday night so we only have about four hours in the afternoon."

"I have to do a little shuffling of our plans tomorrow but I think I can make it. I'll try to be here at one."

LiJing had briefed Marcus on what she had heard from her father relative to the possible shipment, but he was curious to know if Yohana had been told by her father what to expect. As they both went below deck, Marcus said, "Any word from your Dad on what we can expect to transfer?"

"My father called me yesterday and told me to expect to transfer eight and he gave me the GPS coordinates of where to meet the cartel boat. He further told me that, like last time, we would be met by the Avocado launch in Monterey Bay as opposed to going up to the Santa Cruz Marina, which is a good thing. If all goes well and we have good weather for sailing, we could be back way before morning."

That's interesting. LiJing's father indicated there were only to be seven, thought Marcus but he responded, "That's great. It would be nice to get some shut-eye before the day begins. Say, you are dressed sort of casual today. What are we planning to accomplish?"

"The main thing I need your help with is the spinnaker. We may have the opportunity to use it in the next regatta. The last time we used it we didn't pack it properly in its bag to make it easily available when under sail. In fact, it was just pushed down through the hatch into the forward cabin. I'm sure you remember its quite huge."

Saying this she led Marcus forward and opened the door to the very small forward cabin exposing a sea of white sailcloth appearing to fill the whole cabin.

"Marcus, you stay here and I'll go back up on deck and drop down through the forward hatch. That way we can work towards each other stuffing the spinnaker in its bag. Don't start until I get in position. I'm sure its bag is underneath it on the forward bunk."

Reaching under the sail, Marcus found the sail bag and on signal started stuffing. Initially Marcus could not see Yohana who was supposedly collapsing the sail on her end as he stuffed from his end. As the spinnaker was collapsed and stuffed into the bag, the forward cabin cleared exposing the beautiful Yohana lying on the forward bunk totally nude. "Surprise and welcome," she said, continuing her endeavor to tempt Marcus.

Marcus immediately thought, *I guess Jenna was right.*

⟨Φ⟩

Sunday had been planned as another trip to the Aquarium, this time with the Wongs. Jenna's Uncle Mark had agreed to come in and give another tour of the aquarium to Jenna and Marcus as well as the Wongs.

Paramount for the visit was to see the seahorse and the sea otter exhibits as both had been unavailable on Marcus and Jenna's prior visit due to maintenance. Needless to say, Jenna was not happy finding out that Marcus had to go sailing with Yohana again. Marcus had mixed emotions because he really wanted to see the sea otter exhibit. They were discussing this situation Saturday night over cocktails at the Petersons while Sophia and Jenna showed off their purchases from the city.

"Did your Uncle Mark say what time we should be at the aquarium? All I remember is that we're supposed to meet there on Sunday," said Marcus.

"I'm sorry," said Jenna. "I told the Wongs but I didn't tell you. We have to be there early in the morning. He wants to show us around before the Aquarium officially opens. We were planning to go to brunch after the visit."

"Well, that'll work. I can go on the visit," responded Marcus. "I just won't be able to go to brunch. You guys go to brunch and I go to sail. I don't have to be at the marina until 1 o'clock. Juan has a Pebble Beach assignment in the morning and Yohana has to work at the Sardine Factory that evening. We will only have about a four-hour window to practice with *Spirit.*"

Thank God for that, thought Jenna. *At least there won't be any time for her to woo Marcus.* Of course, Jenna had no idea what had happened earlier that day.

CHAPTER 22

MAJOR TRANSFER

T he race course for the regatta was not as long as it has been in the past, but one of the legs allowed for a spinnaker run. Luckily Juan and Marcus had had the chance to practice on the Sunday before.

Critical to a spinnaker run is the beginning and the end. Normally you're coming off a broad reach with the wind and as the yacht is brought fully before the wind, the spinnaker is raised quickly to fill and the jib is dropped. The spinnaker pole is set to the opposite side of the main. This takes two on the bow working as a team. At the completion of a spinnaker run, the same thing is done in reverse and must be accomplished quickly. *Spirit* having a hatch in the bow allowed for the spinnaker to be stuffed directly below as it was dropped. *Spirit* did well on this run, moving ahead of many of the competitive boats. The last leg of the course followed the spinnaker run and put *Spirit* on a beam reach that was headed towards the ocean.

Juan and Marcus smiled and waved at the two motor launches marking the finish and Yohana kept *Spirit* on course towards the ocean instead of turning back towards the marina.

"I believe we really did well," she called out to Marcus and Juan who were still on the forward deck. "Come on back to the cockpit and relax. If the wind holds, we should be able to maintain this course all the way out to the pickup point. I believe it's over 3 miles out. Juan, you can go below and set the pickup point on the GPS screen. We'll have to monitor our location and possibly slow down so we reach the pickup point at about the same time that the Picuda does. I'm sure we will get a radio message from them telling us where they are and when to expect them."

⊕

The sea was calm and *Spirit* arrived at the meeting point early. Marcus and Juan had dropped the sails, and Yohana with the engine on was keeping *Spirit* in tight circles.

Marcus sat on the foredeck with binoculars watching south; Juan was in the pilothouse watching the GPS screen, and had the radio on the channel they expected to hear from the cartel Picuda boat on when they got in range. It was almost simultaneously that Yohana heard Marcus call out, "I have them in sight." and Juan conversing in Spanish with the cartel boat crew.

As the Picuda approached, Yohana called out, "Marcus, you go below. Juan and I, with the cartel boat crew, can handle the transfer. As they come onboard, we'll send the Chinese below. Hearing a welcome and instructions from you in their native language will make them feel comfortable and you can place them in the main cabin as you see fit. It's better they are there during the run into Monterey Bay as it will be dark when we get in there and too dangerous to have them up on deck."

Initially the transfer went smoothly. Marcus welcomed and seated seven Chinese in the main cabin, four at the galley table and three in the lounge area. Then he heard loud yelling on deck in Spanish. It sounded like Yohana was arguing with someone from the cartel crew.

On deck and in Spanish, Yohana said, "I don't want him. Take him back or throw him overboard. He is supposed to be dead."

"You have to take him," said the cartel crewmember.

Then Raul said, "Yohana, I survived, saved by some fishermen. Look, your father sent me to Acapulco to set up the bank account that the cartel can pay us in. You have to take me as I have to report back to your father."

"Raul, I can't trust you. You're a dangerous menace," said Yohana and turning to the cartel crewmember, she said, "Tie him up and stuff him down the forward hatch of my boat. Juan will help you."

Raul cried out, "You can't do this."

And Yohana responded, "I can do whatever I want, Raul. Put some tape on his mouth before you throw him down the forward hatch. I don't want to listen to him."

Once that was accomplished, the Picuda took off at high speed south and Yohana set a course east to Monterey Bay and the general location where they had met the Avocado launch on the last transfer. It was dead calm, thus requiring *Spirit* to continue under engine power. Marcus spent the entire time below in the main cabin chatting with the Chinese engineers and students while Juan was in the pilothouse on the GPS monitor.

Meeting the Avocado launch was a little chancy this trip as it was quite dark and cloudy and no moonlight. In addition to running lights, Yohana turned on the sheet light for the main that is used when sailing in the dark. This lit *Spirit* up pretty well, allowing the Avocado boat to recognize her when they got close. As the Avocado cruiser approached, Yohana called Marcus up on deck to assist with the transfer.

The Avocado crew wasn't quite as adept as the crew on the Picuda; thus the transfer of the seven Chinese took a little bit more time. It was during the transfer that Juan apprised Marcus that Raul was tied up in the forward cabin. "He's a dangerous bastard. Tried to kill me on the last time out. What are we going to do with him?" asked Marcus.

"We will turn him loose when we get back to the Monterey Marina. I'm sure our father will have people there to pick him up," responded Juan.

CHAPTER 23

BACK TO
MONTEREY MARINA

At the completion of the transfer, the Avocado cruiser headed back to Santa Cruz while Yohana set a course south to the Monterey Marina and called out, "Marcus, come back to the cockpit and take the helm for the first shift. Juan, you can go below and get some shut-eye. Oh, before you leave the foredeck, crack the forward hatch a little bit to give our prisoner some air."

Juan went below deck and stretched out on one of the forward bunks in the salon while Yohana followed him down, picked up a blanket and returned to the cockpit, shutting the door to the pilothouse and settling down next to Marcus on his left. "What did you learn from the Chinese?" she asked.

"Well, four of them were software engineers employed by Avocado Corporation at their China operation. The other three are students who were embarking on expense-paid research fellowships at universities. One was headed to Boston to attend the Massachusetts Institute of Technology, the other two were headed locally to the University of California at Berkeley. What was interesting was the students told me that as a requirement to getting their fellowships, they had to join the military and were told that their fellowship would be considered as part of their military service and they be compensated accordingly. They also said that they were told not to mention this when they registered at the universities."

"I'm surprised they told you that," said Yohana. "They consider me and you and Juan as part of the cartel and therefore not connected any way officially to the US."

"Well, that's all fascinating but I'm going to try to get some rest while you keep us on course," Yohana said as she snuggled up to Marcus.

⟨⊕⟩

It was about an hour and a half out. Yohana was fast asleep next to Marcus in the cockpit and Juan, asleep below deck was woken by a tapping noise coming from the door to the forward cabin. He thought *that must be Raul kicking the door with his foot. I wonder what his problem is. He's tied up so I guess I can open the door and check it out.*

As he opened the door, Raul, lying on top of the bundled spinnaker on top of the bunk, slid out of the cabin and onto the floor. Juan, pulling the tape off Raul's face, said, "What's your problem?"

"I have to pee," said Raul.

"Okay, the door to the head is right here. I'll help you stand up and help you in there. Your hands are tied in front of you so you should have no problem." With that said, Juan helped Raul into the head and closed the door. What he didn't know was that Raul had loosened the rope tying his hands and was holding his hands together with the rope appearing to be tied.

Raul relieved himself and proceeded to untie his feet. He then knocked on the door signaling Juan that he had finished and was ready to be helped out. As Juan approached the door turning the lever to open it, Raul pushed on the other side with all his might. The door swung open hitting Juan and knocking him down. Raul, quickly exiting the head, hit Juan with his fist hard enough to knock him unconscious and proceeded back into the forward cabin.

With the door to the pilothouse closed and the engine running, Marcus was totally oblivious to what was going on below deck. With the forward hatch being partially open, Raul was able to open it all the way with minimum noise. The view of the hatch from the cockpit was obstructed due to the main and mizzen masts. That, coupled with there being no moon, total darkness prevailed, allowing Raul to climb up on deck unobserved by Marcus, whose primary focus was on the binnacle.

Raul held a small colt junior .25 ACP pistol that he had strapped to his leg and due to their haste was undetected by the cartel crew that tied him up and pushed him down into the forward cabin. He slowly moved along the port side of the deck holding onto the main boom with his free hand. As he approached the cockpit, he was partially shielded by the pilothouse. Standing at the end of the pilothouse pointing his gun at Marcus he startled him and woke up Yohana by calling out, "Such a sweet couple, it's a shame that one of you is about to die." Then he pulled the trigger. Before the gun went off, Yohana yelled, "No" and jumped in front of Marcus, deflecting Raul's shot. The bullet went through her left arm.

Meanwhile, Juan had recovered consciousness and had climbed out on deck through the forward hatch. Rushing to the cockpit, he pushed Raul from behind, sending them crashing into the binnacle as he yelled, "You bastard, you shot my sister." Raul dropped his gun and hit his head on the binnacle, falling to the cockpit floor.

Marcus set the auto pilot, knelt down to Yohana and called out to Juan, "Go below and get the first aid kit. She will be okay. It appears the bullet went through her muscle and didn't hit a bone or artery. But we've got to apply antiseptic and a bandage to prevent infection and superficial bleeding. I'm not sure about Raul. He appears to be unconscious and has a horrible gash in his forehead."

⟨ᗡ⟩

After bandaging Yohana and Raul, Juan and Marcus retied Raul and locked him again in the forward cabin. They put Yohana in the aft master cabin and gave her a sedative that was in the first aid kit.

Spirit had maintained a fairly straight course because it was still on auto pilot and the sea was calm. Juan took the helm, taking *Spirit* off auto pilot and continued on a course heading to Monterey Marina. Being too far out for cell service, Marcus radioed the Coast Guard. He explained the situation and asked them to put him through to FBI Agent José Rodriguez, giving them his phone number.

There were several rings before a somewhat groggy Rodriguez answered. Marcus responded, "Good morning, José. Sorry to wake you so early but I have a serious issue. It's critical that you get word to Yohana's father at the federal prison. He should be informed immediately that she has been shot by Raul. This will definitely upset him and I'm sure he will have members of his organization meet us at the Marina and pick up Raul. We are about an hour and a half out. If that happens, Juan and I will be able to secure *Spirit* and I'll take Yohana to an urgent care facility when they open. I'll explain it was just an accidental shooting that occurred while she was cleaning the gun we keep for repelling sharks. I want to be able to maintain our undercover operation and I think we can do that by not involving you officially and/or the local police."

"Marcus, I don't understand. What's happened?"

I'm sorry, José. I just got ahead of myself. Let me explain." Marcus then quickly explained all that had happened and ended the call by urging Jose to proceed as quickly as possible.

⊕

As they approached the Monterey breakwater, they dropped the speed of *Spirit* way down as the Monterey fishing fleet boats were leaving the harbor. One of the fishing boats headed straight for *Spirit*. Marcus at the helm called Juan who was down below tending to Yohana, saying,

"Juan, one of the boats is heading this way and they're calling your name over a megaphone."

Juan raced up to the cockpit and seeing the boat heading their way, ran out to the bow. Marcus put *Spirit's* engine in reverse briefly to slow it down. As the two boats drifted together a line was passed from the fishing boat, which Juan secured. Two men on the forward deck of the fishing boat called over to Juan in Spanish, saying, "We understand you have a piece of shit aboard that your father wants us to pick up. Can we help you with it?"

"Si," responded Juan and then calling back to Marcus, he said, "Hold firm, they are taking Raul."

They then stepped over on to *Spirit* while Juan opened the forward hatch. Raul was then quickly transported over to the fishing boat. Juan unsecured the line holding the boats together and the fishing boat quickly motored away. Turning back to Marcus, he said, "I believe that's the last we will hear or see of that piece of shit."

"Good! Come take the helm while I call Jenna to come down and meet us. We need to get Yohana to an urgent care facility as quickly as possible," responded Marcus.

CHAPTER 24

CELEBRATION

Dawn was just breaking as *Spirit* approached the dock in Monterey Marina. Juan and Marcus were happy to see Jenna and Jack Wong on the dock.

"Welcome home," called out Jenna. "Where's the patient?"

"We gave her a sedative and she's down below asleep in the forward cabin," responded Marcus. "We'll wake her up after we're tied up. She only has a flesh wound in her left arm so she should be fine and mobile when we wake her up. Are there any urgent care facilities close by and open?"

"There's one over in Seaside and I believe it's open 6 to 6. I'll take her there," responded Jenna.

"Juan, I think it best that you go with your sister. Jack and I can secure *Spirit* and lock her up."

"Thanks, Marcus. She's covered on my insurance as Pebble Beach offered better coverage than what she could get at the Sardine Factory. I don't know if she's got her card in her purse, but I've got mine. Also, I think I can tell a convincing story about the accidental gunshot that occurred onboard with our shark protection gun. It would be best if we could avoid them reporting it to the police."

"I agree to that," responded Marcus as he also thought *if they reported to the police, I would have to get Rodriguez involved to square things away, and that would blow my cover. I'm not sure we want to do that just yet.*

As soon as they had tied *Spirit* up, Juan went below and woke up Yohana, telling her that Jenna was going to take them both to urgent care to get her wound dressed and get her some antibiotics. Her first words were, "Where's that bastard Raul?"

"Not to worry. Dad sent two men from the mob out to pick him up. They came out on one of the fishing boats before we even got to the marina. I don't think we'll have to deal with him ever again."

⟐

It was a bit of a drive over to Seaside. Yohana was in the front seat with Jenna and Juan in the back. Yohana proceeded to tell Jenna what all happened and how she had jumped in front of Marcus to keep him from getting shot by Raul. Juan then jumped into the conversation, telling how he neutralized Raul and what they did with him.

As they pulled into the parking lot of the Urgent Care facility, Jenna was totally surprised when Yohana reached over, grabbing her arm, and said, "Jenna, I just wanted to tell you that you are a very lucky lady. The number of times I've tried to seduce your husband, he has never taken the bait. There is no question I like him very much, but he is definitely yours. You take care of him."

Before Jenna could say anything, Yohana had opened the door and she and Juan were on their way in to Urgent Care.

⟐

Marcus was able to set up a conference call with Station Chief Alonzo and José Rodriguez at 1 o'clock in the afternoon. He debriefed them on all that happened on the transfer and further all that he had learned from the seven Chinese who were smuggled in.

Station Chief Alonzo indicated that with that information, he had all he needed to pass on to the FBI. This information coupled with what they were receiving about other avenues conducting importation of Chinese was enough for them to move out nationwide and question companies like Avocado Corporation as well as universities doing research partially funded by the Chinese. He further indicated it was Marcus's call whether he wanted to stay undercover or not. There would certainly be no more transfers locally as the yachting season was over until next spring, and by that time Marcus and Jenna would've left the Presidio and moved on to their next assignment. Rodriguez indicated that he could not move on the local Mexican Mafia as the only information he had was Marcus's word as to what happened and he assumed Marcus would not testify against Yohana.

Station Chief Alonzo also told Marcus to tell LiJing he would be dealing directly with her father in the future. With all that was said, Station Chief Alonzo proclaimed the case locally as officially closed and Marcus could return full time to his studies at the Presidio.

⟨⟩

A lot happened in the weeks that followed.

Their final test occurred at the Presidio. As predicted by LiJing, it was an escape room. This time the suite represented the Raffles Hotel in Singapore complete with the Long Bar. Unfortunately, there were no Singapore Slings to sip. All directions and clues were in a mixture of Mandarin and Malay with a sprinkling of English. Again, Jack Wong and Jenna's team was the first out.

Fall came early to Monterey. The trees along Alvarado Street changed color and dropped their leaves. Jenna loved the sound they made as she kicked and stepped on them when walking down to the wharf for Sunday brunch. It was on just such a walk that Jenna got the idea. "Marcus, I think we ought to have a celebration."

"What do you mean, celebration?"

"We book a dinner party at the yacht club and invite all our friends here. Sort of a bon farewell. We will be leaving soon to go back to New York and probably never see them again. I think we need to get together and tell them how much we enjoyed being with them these past months. It certainly has been exciting, and we have had many pleasurable experiences."

"That's a great idea, Jenna. After brunch this morning we will go over to the yacht club and set it up. You can send out some invitations this afternoon."

⟨⟩

It was a Saturday afternoon. Jenna had reserved the large round table next to the windows in the yacht club. All seven were seated around the table. Two pitchers of margaritas and several appetizers were on the table and conversation was abundant. Coincidentally to set the mood, Jimmy Buffett was singing "Margaritaville" on the club sound system.

Marcus tapped his glass with a spoon and stood up, saying, "We gathered you all together as a sort of jollification and to thank you for how you've affected our lives these last months. Through friendship and camaraderie, we have experienced crises and celebration together."

Jenna then stood up next to Marcus and, looking at the Jones, said, "Uncle Mark, it all started when you greeted us at the hotel. Seeing family when you're checking in at a strange location immediately calms the trepidation we may have experienced. Aunt Susan, those family home-cooked meals were such a nice break."

"Mark, the aquarium tours that you took us on were fantastic. You obviously showed us parts of the aquarium and processes that go on that most visitors never know about. It was all marvelous," added Marcus.

Then turning to the Wongs, he said, "I can't imagine a better couple to have partnered with through this whole activity. Through thick and thin, we were there for each other. It has been really great. And Jack, you learned to sail; I think that was outstanding."

Jenna then said, "Sophia, your stories of Rio were captivating. I sure hope to visit there someday."

And then a little facetiously Marcus added, "And I would like to come along and look up that girl from Ipanema."

"She really did exist, but I think she's long gone now," said Sophia and then she added, "Seriously, who knows, in the future we might all be able to visit there. I still have family in Rio de Janeiro, and I'm sure they'd be happy to host us."

"That could be great," responded Jenna.

Then both Jenna and Marcus looked at LiJing. Marcus said, "LiJing, I don't know how you do it, but you take a very difficult process and make it enjoyable. I have studied under many teachers and professors but none as capable as you. You are truly unique."

"Hear, hear," chimed in the Wongs.

"That is so true," added Jenna.

Then turning to Juan and Yohana, Marcus said, "Yohana, what can I say? Both you and Juan opened a whole new world for us here in Monterey. Sailing on *Spirit* and joining the yacht club provided experiences that one could only dream about. You both are so likeable, terrific to be with and to sail with. And *Spirit* is a marvelous yacht, capable of comfortable cruising as well as competitive yacht racing. Truly we will miss you both so very much,"

Not I, thought Jenna.

Then raising his glass, Marcus said, "Here's to you all. We love you and will miss you. But most of all, we thank you for being most wonderful friends."

◐

Two weeks later they returned to their apartment in New York.

The end.

EPILOGUE

"Marcus, Jenna, report!" The PA system boomed across the cubicles on the 10th floor of the CIA office complex in Manhattan. Some things change and some things never do. Marcus and Jenna's boss still loved the PA system rather than a phone, much to the chagrin of the staff.

"Marcus, Jenna, now!" boomed the PA system again. They both rapidly got up, nearly colliding as they exited their cubicles and rushed to the boss's office.

"Close the door, sit," said the boss. "Now, both of you, relax and listen. Station Chief Alonzo was extremely pleased with what you accomplished in Monterey while attending language school at the Presidio. However, now is the time to prepare for your next operational assignment. The language school was a precursor. You are about to be assigned to Singapore. Again, you will be undercover and teamed as a young married couple. You will be employed by Citibank Singapore. Now that's halfway around the world so you will not be able to commute back to New York. You will be there for an extended stay. I would suggest you get your affairs in order. Give up or lease your apartment. Say your goodbyes to your local relatives. You will be allowed to ship 500 pounds apiece and it will be shipped directly to the US Consulate in Singapore. All other belongings should either be disposed of or stored. Currently, you are scheduled to depart in three weeks. You will be flying from New York to the West Coast and nonstop from the West Coast to Singapore.

Your initial accommodations in Singapore will be prearranged and during the next three weeks you will be attending several security briefings concerning your assignment. I will be available for any questions you have in the interim. If you have none now, you're dismissed."

Before you close the book.

I sincerely hope you enjoyed the story as much as I enjoyed writing it. Jenna and Marcus are destined to have further adventures, and I will do my best to bring them to you.

I, as all writers, wish to get our stories into the hands of as many readers as possible. Therefore, it's critical for you to write a review.

It can be as brief as a few words or several sentences.

But please, now go onto Amazon and write a review.

Thank you.

Larry Andrews

www.larryandrewsnovelist.com

TITLES BY LARRY ANDREWS

A SPACE ODDITY

THE CARIBBEAN ENDEAVOR

TERROR IN TUSCANY

MAYHEM IN MONTEREY

Made in the USA
Monee, IL
02 July 2021

72119784R00092